Path of Fire

T. T. Henderson

INDIGO

Indigo is an imprint of
Genesis Press, Inc.
315 Third Avenue North
Columbus, Mississippi 39701

Path of Fire

ISBN 1-58571-012-1

Manufactured in the United States of America

FIRST EDITION

Thanks to my husband, Alan, for his love and support

And to Mustapha Mansaray for sharing stories about his homeland

Path of Fire

One

Cristiana Algood despised her ex-husband—at least she tried to find a reason to every day. Mason was a dog. A smooth-talkin', good-lookin', skirt-chasin', paper-wettin' canine prince of Washington, DC, who'd divorced her almost a year ago to marry a supermodel.

A supermodel.

Oh, the looks she'd endured from her gossipy family and friends. Tia, being a long way from emaciatingly thin, couldn't endure their pity and well-meaning advice. Especially her Aunt Mae's suggestion to "drop twenty pounds and dress like a two-dollah 'ho'" to get her husband back. Suffering through the humiliation was enough to justify homicidal thoughts, but before she acted on any, she decided it was time to go. To get as far away from Mason as possible.

Only a week ago, she'd kissed her parents good-bye and stolen away to Zaire to heal the wounds of her shattered self-esteem. It seemed like forever.

From her first day in Zaire she'd buried herself in the task of helping the refugees in Uvira. From making meals to treating wounds, Tia assisted the seasoned aid workers with whatever was necessary to help the people survive. And in that short time frame, their problems had become her own. Now she forced her way through a thick mass of panicked Hutus for the sake of her own survival.

"Ow!"

Tia pushed the elbow from her ribs. She couldn't tell who the appendage belonged to because she was being crushed by a mass of bodies.

The sky thundered with mortars and the dock beneath her swung with the weight of hundreds of screaming people. War had come to Uvira, the Hutu refugee camp where Tia worked.

Gunfire rat-a-tatted overhead. Tia and the refugees ducked before renewing efforts to reach the lone boat at the dock. Her boat—provided by the Feed The World Foundation to get relief workers out of the country. Not sweaty, panicking refugees, she thought with mounting irritation.

"Excuse me!" she shouted. "I need to get through here!"

If anyone heard her over their own cries, they ignored her. Hot, scared and desperate to get home, Tia was losing patience. She wedged her arm between herself and the damp back of the man in front of her. Her push brought a scowl of warning from the man and no progress forward.

An explosion rumbled the air above Tia's head and a veil of smoke clouded her vision. She swallowed a throatful of fear and ducked to avoid debris.

Until now, the closest she'd been to guns was at her father's annual skeet shoot competitions. At the time, she'd had no clue how destructive weapons could be. Watching a clay puck scatter against a pristine blue sky was a far cry from witnessing a bullet shatter a man's skull.

Shuddering, she squeezed her eyes closed and tried to erase the memory of Tutsi bullets ripping through the camp, hitting this Hutu man, missing another. She'd dodged several prone bodies an hour ago, and with bloody shards of bone clinging to her T-shirt, she'd raced the bullets with horror-fueled urgency.

She'd be running still if it hadn't been for this human traffic jam at the dock. She didn't blame them for wanting out of this country—couldn't. But she wished like hell they'd get out of her way.

The panicked cries, along with the hot, humid air she sucked in, nauseated Tia and weakened her efforts forward. Her stomach shifted with weird convulsions so that she prayed to keep her meager lunch down, certain that the tall man jumping and waving in front of her would do more than frown if she showered him with vomit.

Tired of pushing forward only to be shoved backward, Tia gave up the struggle. She allowed the crowd to move her left and right like a piece of driftwood on the sea. A sea of body odor, heat and frenzy. Her eyes felt heavy, her head fuzzy. Technicolor stars danced behind her tightly squeezed lids as her personal space diminished.

Her stomach roiled threateningly. Her knees wobbled. If she fell, she'd be trampled in this herd of humanity. Panic brought clarity to her mind and determination to her feet.

"Come on, Tia," she said to herself as she opened her eyes. "It's only a few more steps."

Craning her neck, she tried to look past the heads of the refugees surrounding her. At the end of the dock was her transport out of Zaire. It was only a few precious feet...and a thousand bodies away.

The boat's engine roared, signaling its intent to leave. Michael Van Horn, a fellow relief worker, stood at the back of the boat with his hands cupped to his mouth. "Hurry, Tia!" he seemed to be shouting. He clung to the railing of the boat, waving his Feed The World baseball cap to catch her attention.

In a less tense situation, she would've laughed. He didn't have to wave; all he had to do was stand still and be white. His pale skin stood out amongst the hundreds of stowaways like the creme filling of an Oreo cookie. Then she saw a man untie a rope from the dock and struggle to regain his place inside the boat.

They were leaving without her! "Pardon me!" Her words were buried under the din.

Tia wedged her girth between two tall Hutu men and pushed with all her might.

An arm dug into her back. A large foot crushed her toes. "Damn," she muttered. She'd just spent the last week helping these people and now they were keeping her from getting home.

At least I have a home to go to.

The sobering thought put her anger in check. Sadness for the refugee's plight had brought her to Zaire. But now, fear for her own life made her anxious to leave. Did that make her selfish or sane?

"No time for philosophical questions, Tia," she spoke aloud. "You've got to make it to that boat." Just saying the words seemed to help.

Tia put her head down and her elbows out like a football player needing yardage. For once, her extra weight proved beneficial. Men and women were forced to the side as she pushed herself through the throng. Exhausted, panting, she gave one final thrust.

With a mighty grunt, she fought her way to fresh air, daylight... and the edge of an empty dock. The boat, packed with four hundred or so Hutus and aid workers, was several yards out in the lake and pitching from side to side.

"Wait!" she shouted. "Don't leave me!"

Desperately, Hutu after Hutu threw themselves off the creaking wood, attempting to swim for the boat. Tia planted her feet and watched, not daring to do the same. Her swimming left much to be desired and she'd never catch the boat. Suddenly, someone hit her left arm, throwing her off balance. She circled her arms in the air and teetered on the tip of one expensive hiking boot for a second before falling face first into the murky waters of the Tanganyika.

The lake swallowed her whole, despite the thrashing of her legs and arms. Realizing her backpack was weighing her down, she wriggled her arms free of the Doone and Bourke original, electing to drag it instead. The darn thing had a duck on it, why wasn't it more buoyant?

Her lungs were on the verge of bursting when she hit the surface. Taking a huge gulp of air, she squinted against the splashing all around her. A few men and boys had been fast enough to reach the retreating vessel, but refugees hanging to the sides of the boat beat them back into the water.

Tia felt nauseous. And lonely. And a lot like Dorothy from the Wizard of Oz. Thrashing about as best she could, she struggled to shore, wishing desperately for a pair of ruby slippers. Spitting out a mouthful of nasty water, she pulled herself up the slick bank to the narrow strip of sand.

Dragging her backpack behind her, she crawled like a sand crab to the miserly shelter of a wide rock. There were no slippers, no good fairy ...

"Hey, hey, hey, Tia."

She turned just in time to catch the three-year-old boy as he dove into her arms. Here was a munchkin if she ever saw one.

"Hey, Denis." She caught the dark child and hugged him tightly. His thick mat of hair grazed her cheek and he smelled of little boy sweat.

She sighed and looked into the eyes of the child's father, Fidele Zavi, who'd chased after him. "I thought you were gone," she said.

"We saw your lovely dive off the dock," Fidele teased in a low whisper as he dove behind the rock beside her. "Did you choose not to swim to Tanzania, after all?"

"Don't start with me, Fidele," she cautioned. It was an awkward conversation with both of them watching warily for the Tutsi rebels who were raining fire on them. "I'm stranded, and I'm not happy."

Denis giggled and hugged Tia's neck tighter, not caring that he was getting as soaked as she.

Pushing aside irritation, she returned the boy's affection. In her arms she held the best and the worst part of Zaire. This Hutu child had grown up in a refugee camp, not knowing what it felt like to have solid walls around him. The only thing his parents had been able to give him was temporary safety from guns—and the stability of their love.

Stability? Love? Were the words even remotely related? She'd joined the Feed The World Foundation in Washington, DC, hoping to put as many miles between herself and her ex-husband, Mason, as possible. How typical of him to reach across the world to slap her in the face with the telegram of his new wife's successful delivery of an heir.

Tia hugged the boy tighter in remembrance of the babies she'd miscarried. Just thinking about Mason as father to someone else's baby hurt to her soul. If not for the danger, she would remain a while longer in Zaire. She wasn't sure if she was ready to face her own world yet.

Rapid shots, like vicious Fourth of July fireworks, broke limbs and shredded leaves behind them. Tia pushed the child to the sand and covered him with her body. Her heart rate refused to slow down even when the shooting stopped. Wiping sand from her mouth, she peered cautiously around her.

Rising up to check the boy, Tia saw the wide giggling grin he offered her and her heart nearly broke. "Bless your heart, Denis."

Leave it to a child to laugh when his life was in danger. All too soon he'd know the difference. Until then, who was she to tell him any different?

"Tia," his wide brown eyes danced with merriment. "You come with us."

"Come with you, Denis?"

"Yes." Fidele, now serious, brushed sand from his pants. "It'll be safer if you come with us to Kigali."

Looking at the thinning crowd on the dock, Tia knew he was right. If she waited for another boat to appear, she'd be caught in the crossfires of war. "Is it far?" she asked Fidele.

"Far enough," he nodded. "But, once across the Rwandan border, we can get you to an American embassy."

She squinted up at the dark African man. "I guess I don't have much choice." Turning her attention back to Denis, she continued to speak to him in French, the language he understood as well as his native tongue. "Well Denis, my friend. I guess I'm coming with you."

The boy's celebration ended quickly when gunfire once again punctuated the sky above them. Tia and Fidele hunched over the boy protectively.

"We must leave quickly." Fidele pulled Denis into his arms and headed down the beach at a trot.

Despite wet clothing, a full sweat broke out on Tia's forehead in the short time it took to reach the edge of the forest. Huffing to catch her breath, she lamented not having dropped a few pounds. Of course, it wasn't like she hadn't tried...a few thousand times.

Mortar shells pounded the earth and quickened their movements. Fidele Zavi met up with his wife Sarini and their eight children and sped into the dense jungle. Tia was afraid to follow and terrified not to. Each booming mortar explosion had her ducking and dodging the resultant shower of sand, plants and dirt.

"C'mon, Tia." Denis reached out a thin arm over his father's shoulder. "Hu-wee."

Encouraged along by the determined three-year-old, she made her way down the narrow path into the jungle. The bush.

Goosebumps rose on the back of her neck as she followed the Zavis, shielding her face from the huge, slapping leaves of eight foot tall plants. She didn't like feeling closed in, yet each step took her deeper and deeper into the belly of the jungle. Only the fear of bullets allowed her to lay aside her claustrophobia and press onward.

A tangle of tree branches that seemed to soar as high as the sky itself blocked the Zairian sun and permitted only glimpses of light to pass through their collective branches.

It was so hot and muggy, Tia couldn't tell if her clothes had ever dried, because sweat kept them clinging to her.

By dusk, Tia's legs were wobbly and she was drunk with exhaustion. Thankfully, they reached a clearing and Tia stopped. "Fidele." She slumped against a tree.

She could barely distinguish his slight figure in the diminishing light, but she knew he continued walking.

"Fidele!"

The Zavis and dozens of other refugees stopped to look at her.

"Yes, Tia?" he called back. "What is it?"

"Can we stop now?" Her legs wouldn't last much longer and her stomach rumbled from inattention. "Please?"

Fidele made much ado about scanning the area. "This will do." He walked ahead, gaining the attention of the other men. A few of the Zavi children patted her gratefully on the arm. They too needed to rest, but would not say so to their father. It would've been disrespectful.

Tia sent a silent prayer of thanks upward and forced her legs to move far enough to join them. Fidele left the other men in the group. Once all had agreed to stop for the night, the women began preparing dinner.

Their meal was meager. Sarini and the others dispensed cold canned beans and high protein crackers they'd taken from the food storehouse. Each person had a single cup of fresh water to wash it down.

Tia gave her spoon a final lick, though it was cleaner than when she'd started. Her stomach didn't feel anywhere near full. Unfortunately, she was subject to the same rationing as her traveling companions. And here in Zaire, there was no such thing as seconds.

Darkness descended quickly in the jungle. Stories of the day were told as they all sat in a circle around a discreet fire, not wanting to draw unnecessary attention to their location. Tia closed her eyes against the keening of women who'd lost husbands, sons, and daughters that day. Solemn voices rose to fill the sky as the Hutus sang of their grief and anger.

Tia studied the small huddle of Fidele and his children. She'd been here a week, yet knew nothing about these people. This wasn't the first time she'd sat to join them for dinner, but it was the first time she'd had to share in their fear. Fear for their lives.

"Fidele?" She leaned back against a tree, watching the man as he covered his exhausted wife with a worn wool blanket.

"Yes?" His eyes looked around warily before settling on Tia."

"How did this happen? How did you become a refugee?"

Fidele pulled a stick from the ground and began to chew it. Legs folded, he stared into the fire before speaking. "I used to be a civil servant with the Hutu government two years ago. Back when Rwanda was ruled by Hutus."

His head dropped. "I worked with the schools, making sure we had adequate books and teachers, enough chairs for the children. I requested money when new schools were needed." He fell silent for a few moments.

"You speak English very well. And French. I heard you speaking it with the other men," Tia added, appreciating how well he and his family communicated with her.

"Yes. In our schools we teach Kinyarwanda, English and French, our official languages. It makes it easier because every tribe has their own language. And because of our history."

"History?" Tia pulled her wool blanket over her legs against the sudden chill in the humid night air.

"Rwanda, Burundi and Zaire were colonized by the Belgians after World War II until 1962. They are, as you know, a French speaking people. Our main exports are coffee and tea, so we need to trade in English as well. Our cities and schools are of European design. Many of the children are mixed with Belgian blood and many of us carry French or English names as a result of their culture mingling with our own."

"That explains a lot." Tia had expected everyone to have an unpronounceable name when she'd reached Zaire. Many were. But a fair amount, like Fidele, had European names that were quite easy for her to manage. Tia's college-taught French was rough, but she understood snatches of conversations when the other women spoke. It still wasn't clear why a learned couple like Fidele and Sarini were homeless and wandering the Zairian border.

"Rwanda and Zaire are ruled by Africans now, right?"

Fidele nodded. "Unfortunately, despite all efforts to democratize our government, our rulers are determined by coups, not elections. Which is why I am now a refugee."

"Because the Tutsis took power in Rwanda?"

"Precisely." He looked at her then. "You see, if your tribe is in power, you have privilege. You get a good job, you can afford a nice house, not one made of thatch and mud. But when another tribe takes control, you lose everything. Sometimes even your life."

"The Tutsis ran you out of Rwanda like we were just run out of Uvira?"

He nodded.

Tia shivered, thinking about how close to death she'd been on the beach. "I probably would've died if not for you, Fidele," Tia said quietly. "Thanks for bringing me along."

His eyes grew wide. "What else could I have done?"

Tia shrugged. "I don't know. I guess you could've left me."

Fidele gave a short laugh and shook his head. "Americans."

The fire died down to glowing red embers after a while, until only a sliver of moon cast an eerie light through the tangled vines and foliage around them. Fidele withdrew to the comfort of the blanket where his wife lay. He threw a large plastic tarp over the majority of his family before settling under it himself. "Go to sleep, Tia. We have a long walk ahead of us tomorrow."

Tia tried to make herself comfortable on the spongy ground. "Oooh," she wailed pitifully while stretching her aching legs.

"Y'okay?" Denis rose from between his parents, rubbing his eyes.

Tia laid a hand on his warm, smooth cheek and smiled at him. "Nothing a good soak in a hot tub wouldn't cure."

"Hot tub?"

"Never mind." She tucked the boy beside her and felt around in her backpack for dessert. "There isn't a situation that a positive outlook and piece of candy can't make better," she told him.

What had it taken her...a whole box of Ghirardelli's and a pint of Ben and Jerry's ice cream to digest Mason's request for a divorce?

She located the Ziploc bag containing lifesavers. Along with it was an envelope. Why she'd kept it was a mystery. It hurt whenever she read it. And now, just thinking of its contents made her heart ache again.

"What's that?" Denis asked.

Swallowing hard, Tia crumpled the birth announcement for Mason Drew Algood II. Figures he'd name the child after himself. "Trash." She tossed it aside. "I should've thrown it away when I first got it."

Mason had asked for their divorce. So why didn't he just move on with his new life, his new wife, his new baby, without taking every opportunity to tell Tia how great everything was going for him?

Why was he going so far out of his way to make her miserable?

"Y'okay?" Denis put a hand to her cheek.

Tia kissed his dirty fingers and pulled him closer. "Yeah. I'll be fine." After all, nothing Mason could do was worse than almost dying, she reassured herself. Remembering her mission, she unwrapped two pieces of candy and handed one to her small friend. "Shhh. Be very quiet and try not to bite. It'll last longer," she instructed.

Denis nodded and popped the round delicacy in his mouth. Tia laughed at his bulging cheek.

"Thish ish goot," Denis smiled.

Her little slice of heaven lasted only a few precious moments, but Tia felt a lot better. Using her backpack as a pillow, she lay down on the hard ground, thankful she was too exhausted to worry about how uncomfortable the night was going to be or how far Washington, DC, was from here.

At least tonight's lullaby wasn't the sound of gunfire and mortars. They'd either walked far enough away not to hear it, or the Zairian soldiers and Tutsi rebels were taking a break. In their place, the jungle creatures made strange and unsettling night music and the spicy, moldy scent of the jungle filled the air. She lay on the hard earth and jumped at each new sound. It seemed hours before her long walk and shaking fits made her exhausted enough to sleep.

A cool, almost wet, sensation at her ear brought Tia to a semi-conscious state of awareness. She pushed at the object irritably as sunlight stabbed at her closed eyelids. Fatigue still weighed heavy in her bones. She wasn't ready to start a new day yet. The last one had been bad enough.

The cold weight rolled down her neck and let out a distinct hiss. Tia's eyes flew open. A scream froze in her throat. Not daring to breathe or move, Tia silently willed the creature to go away.

As if taking offense to her thoughts, the snake wagged a forked tongue inches from her eyes.

Her heart stopped but didn't have the grace to make her pass out.

Shifting its head left and right, the asp seemed to be deciding which direction to take. Tia didn't much care as long as it left her immediate vicinity without taking a bite of her for breakfast.

Though she wanted to scream and run, she dared not to do either. Tia suffered for a moment past eternity until the snake pulsed and slid its way across her neck onto the jungle floor. Relief flooded her senses, making stars float in dazed circles before her.

Only after the snake stuck its head beneath some leaves a few yards away did Tia dare speak. "Fidele," she whispered hoarsely.

The Hutu man stopped packing his meager gear and gave her a quizzical frown.

"Look." She pointed as she rose from the ground slowly, not wanting the creature to take notice of her again.

Fidele moved closer to the snake as it slithered completely beneath the foliage. "It's not poisonous." He gave her a thoughtful look. "But there's an identical one that is."

"Great." Tia had harbored some unrealistic hope that there were no more such creatures in the jungle. "I don't care if they're not poisonous. How do I keep them away from me?" she asked, shakily.

"Here. Take this." Fidele handed her a long, thin stick with strangely patterned bark. "In the dark, it looks like a red-tongued adder," he explained. "A rival of that black and brown one you just saw."

"Oh. So, it'll scare them away?" Tia tested the weight of the stick.

"No, but it'll attack it instead of you."

Tia imagined snakes falling out of trees to engage the stick in combat. She threw it down quickly. Her heart pounded as she checked nearby branches.

Fidele's shoulders shook as he choked on his laughter.

Realizing she was the brunt of a joke, she glared at the dark man. "Very funny, Fidele." She grabbed her back-pack and followed after him. "I could've had a heart attack, you know." She tried to sound angry, but failed when his infectious giggling got to her. It was his great sense of humor that had made them fast friends earlier in the week. Undoubtedly, his ability to look at life with humor had kept him going during difficult times. Difficult. Heck, this was insanity.

Leaning on a tree, Tia watched Fidele. He wasn't a tall man, nor were any of the Hutus really. She could look him in the eyes without tilting her head. His short crop of tight curls sat well back from his smooth, dark face and when he smiled, his high cheekbones, white teeth and pointed chin gave him the look of a dark elf. Right now he was instructing his children on how to walk on the upcoming paths. They were slippery, he cautioned. They must keep as close to the wall of the mountain as possible. His hand stroked his wife's back in an effort to comfort and strengthen her for the long trek.

Tia's heart gave a lonely pull as she witnessed the caring gesture. She clung to his words, to his optimism, as did his children and several of the other families standing nearby.

"We must look out for each other. If one falls, pick them up. The stronger supports the weaker. We will reach the bottom of this mountain together, and then we shall make our way home." Fidele's eyes moved from one face to another to drive home his point. "Let us begin," he said as his gaze finally rested on Tia.

Despite the aching of her joints and the heaviness of fatigue in her muscles, Tia was bolstered by Fidele's drive. She fell in behind his family, determined to keep up. Soon, she would be home.

But the trek was long. Tia's resolve weakened day by day as she grew more and more tired. Each night, when she managed to fall asleep, she'd toss restlessly, troubled by her dreams

The fourth night, she dreamed again of the asp, that it fell hissing out of a tree onto her. She screamed. Denis dragged his sleepy body over to Tia and lay down beside her. Groggily he patted her cheek with his tiny palm and told her it was just a "bad deem" and to "go asleep."

Sarini lifted troubled eyes in Tia's direction. "Again?" she questioned quietly.

"Yes," Tia nodded. Sarini believed that snake dreams foretold of death. Without another word, she lay back to stare at the stars.

Tia pulled the toddler in close to kiss his fuzzy head. Perhaps because he was the youngest of the Zavi children, or because he represented something she couldn't have, Tia loved Denis dearly. Oddly enough, the warmth of his tiny body calmed her. She reminded herself that she didn't believe in weird stuff like dream predictions and allowed a peaceful sleep to take her.

Two

Joseph stood mired in the early morning mist at the top of the mountain. Was this like heaven, he wondered? Cool, quiet, calm? He closed his eyes and imagined himself there. Imagined his brothers and sisters, his father and his mother all floating toward him with smiles on their faces, welcoming him back to the family.

The grunting and tussling of nearby gorillas forced his eyes open. His temporary happiness faded as he found himself standing alone on the mountain, once again.

"Two years," he spoke aloud. It had been two years since he'd raced away from his graduate studies at Howard University in America to make the exhausting trip home to Rwanda. Three days of planes and boats and buses only to find himself too late to help his family. Hundreds of thousands of Tutsis had been killed in President Habyarimana's "ethnic cleansing" push. It hadn't been safe for Joseph to go home until the President had been killed and the Tutsi tribe controlled Rwanda once again. He'd joined Laurent Kabila's rebellion as a soldier for the Front Patriotique Rwandais soon after.

He squeezed his eyes tight against the unwanted images of his destroyed home and murdered family.

"This is why you fight, Joseph," he told himself. "This is why all Hutus must die."

Descending the high path to his men, he ordered them awake. "We'll continue down the mountain from our higher vantage point and we should be able to cut off the Hutus below by mid-day," he spoke to them in French, the language they all understood best. "Don't attack until we weed out the Hutu militia among them."

"What difference does it make?" Leonard Bolongo, his second-in-command questioned. "A Hutu is a Hutu. I say kill them all."

"Eventually. But let us kill the ones with guns first." Joseph dismissed them irritably. He was growing concerned about Leonard's reckless approach to battle. How many times did he have to remind the man that planning was key when they were so heavily outnumbered?

Joseph didn't know exactly how many Hutus they'd run out of Uvira, but he knew there were at least a hundred on the lower path of the mountain. And one foreigner. A woman with skin the color of a golden sunset and untidy coils of raven hair. He couldn't put her out of his mind. Yet, he had to. Distractions would only put his unit in danger.

Corralling the Hutus at the base as they descended the path seemed the best way to ensure their complete annihilation. "Ethnic cleansing," he said between clenched teeth. "We'll see how they like it."

He'd order his men to let the woman live, however.

It seemed Tia had just closed her eyes when the light of morning breathed a new day into the jungle. Tia's body rebelled against the lack of sleep. The blisters on her feet added to her discomfort. It was as if someone had stuck a hot poker through her shoes and ripped the skin from her big toes and heels.

She decided not to remove her boots, certain that she wouldn't be able to get them back on. Enviously, she watched the Hutus, especially the children, walk barefoot around their small camps. Of course, they had calluses from years of such behavior and Tia wasn't certain the trade-off would be worth it.

An irritable rumbling in the pit of her stomach reminded Tia of her inadequate dinner. She hobbled to where Sarini and her children sat eating steamed rice. Fidele's wife was dark-skinned with lovely features. Her normally bright eyes drooped today. She looked as tired as Tia felt. "You look like ten miles of bad road, home-girl." Tia tried to keep her voice light even though pain permeated every muscle in her body. She eased down beside the woman.

Shaking her head slowly, Sarini closed her eyes. "I don't think I make it to Kigali." Her English was thick with accent and exhaustion.

"Yes, you will," Tia said reflexively. "I know exactly how you feel, but we can't give up."

"I'm tired." Sarini let a lone tear drop from her eye.

Moving in to hug her, Tia sympathized. "Me too. But we'll make it." She closed her eyes wearily. "We have to."

Her mother always accused her of believing in lost causes—a happy marriage to Mason being the most notable. Having a baby was a close second. She hoped this wouldn't be another situation where her faith smashed up against the brick wall of harsh reality.

Tia noticed the men huddled together at the bottom of a steep hill. "What are they doing?" she asked.

Shoving away her tears, Sarini sniffed and looked in the direction Tia pointed. "They not sure which path to take," she explained. "There," she indicated some men high up in the trees, "they try to locate right way so we don't get lost."

"Great," Tia said more to herself than to her companion. Her feet throbbed inside their leather-encased prisons. "For your sake and my blisters, I hope they pick the quickest path."

Attending to her stomach's needs, Tia portioned rice into a bowl. No butter, no sugar—just rice. It didn't taste like much, but at least it put something in her stomach.

The men came to a decision and the journey resumed. Day five of their trek was even more miserable than the first four. Tia followed Sarini, whose steps had slowed considerably. They alternated carrying Denis between them for several hours until Fidele, noting their tortured faces, took the boy himself.

Halfway through the day, Tia's physical discomfort hit a new low. Cursing the unnatural October heat, she blew down the front of her tank top, trying to simulate a cool breeze. The motion of dropping her head increased the throbbing ache that pushed against her sweating temples and made her instantly remorseful.

Hands to her head, she tried to keep the pain from exploding her skull. The aching eased enough for her feet to remind her how badly abused they were.

She'd stopped caring how stupid she must look walking on the sides of her boots. Keeping weight off her toes and heels made it bearable to continue.

What good were two hundred dollar boots if they killed your feet when you used them the way they were meant to be used?

Tia barely lifted her feet from the ground, she couldn't stand the shooting pain when she reapplied pressure with each step.

Sweat trickled down her face, tickling as it made its way to her chin. Swiping irritably at the clinging droplets, Tia prayed for rain. Suddenly, her shuffling feet connected with a protruding vine in the path. Tia went over the edge, the air knocked from her lungs as she connected with the ground. Tumbling at first, then sliding, Tia fell down the mountainside.

Screaming, she turned onto her belly, clawing at the moss, leaves and narrow branches. In turn, the mountain attacked her thighs, belly and breasts. "Fidellle! Helllp!" Dirt and grass filled her mouth as she scrambled to get a foothold—a handhold—on anything as gravity pulled her down.

Her left toe hit something solid and held.

"Thank you, thank you," she spat between breaths. She praised God, whatever was holding her up, grateful the death slide had ceased. Quickly, she dug her right foot into the side of the mountain to better anchor herself. She squeezed debris and tears from her eyes and wrapped her fingers around a thick root in front of her.

Balancing precariously, she listened to her panicked breaths against the indifferent mound of earth beneath her.

Denis's terrified screams sounded far above her. Not daring to look up or down, she pressed herself closer to the moss and dirt and prayed to God to save her.

"Hold on, Tia," Fidele shouted. "Help is coming."

"Good." Tia tried to breathe normally. "Good. They're sending help." She spoke to calm herself as broken grass sailed past in the breeze. "Everything's going to be fine."

Just to defy her positive thinking, her right foot slipped free. Whimpering, she clung to the vine in desperation. Her fingers slipped. She readjusted them. Kicking at the slope, she tried to lodge her foot again.

The grass was still slick with dew. Dear God, it wouldn't stay.

Her hands slipped down the vine again, causing the plant to dig into her fingers. She couldn't hang on much longer. "Help. Oh, help," she cried pitifully.

"Take my hand," a deep voice ordered.

Looking up, Tia made out a dark, muscular arm reaching for her. "I can't." She was afraid to let go of the vine. "I'll fall."

"No. You won't." The man's voice rang of forced patience. "Try."

Not a good idea to argue with a man trying to save your life, she decided. He might change his mind.

Biting her bottom lip, she released the vine with her right hand and reached for his arm. Tia's left foot skidded from its narrow perch and she swung down and away from her would-be savior.

Hot tears blurred her eyes. She couldn't reach him.

Desperately, she reached for the vine, grasping it with both hands again. Tia's arms burned with the strain of holding up all of her hundred and sixty-five pounds.

"Try again!" the man demanded.

"I can't." Tia riled against the authority in his voice. How dare he tell her what to do? Her life was her own. For about two seconds longer.

She gave out a small cry as the vine slipped further from her grasp. Her fingertips throbbed angrily. Tears streamed down her cheeks as she resigned herself to the inevitable.

"Don't give up!" It sounded like an order as he moved closer to her.

"Screw you," she sobbed, wondering if it was the strange man she cursed, or God, who'd abandoned her. The last of the vine slipped through her fingers.

A hand enclosed her wrist like a vise. Shocked, Tia looked up. An ebony man with a magnificently stern expression stared deep into her eyes. "Climb to me," he said. His bass-heavy voice boomed like thunder.

Nodding with renewed hope, Tia immediately repented to the Almighty for her hasty loss of faith. She scrambled up the mountain as the man pulled her to his side.

"Move in front of me. Place both hands on the rope and pull," he ordered once again.

Tia did as she was told. His solid thighs behind her own and the strong beat of his heart against her back reassured her.

"Walk with me." His deep voice was intimate as his hot breaths warmed her ear.

Tia, fueled by adrenaline, began to walk up the slick slope. Men atop the mountain pulled as they climbed. Men who looked no bigger than rats. It frightened Tia all over again to realize how far she'd fallen.

What had taken a few seconds to fall down took an eternity to climb up again. But whenever she weakened, the man behind her would pull for them both. "You can do it," he told her in a calm, encouraging tone as they continued upward. Once at the top, Tia planted her feet solidly on the path and leaned against the man in relief. "Thank you," she said breathlessly against his chest. "Thank you so much."

Joseph Desiré held the woman tightly, knowing her shaking knees weren't up to the job. Her "thank you" had been spoken in English with a decidedly American accent. He'd guessed right. She was a tourist.

As foreign as her dialect, was the weight of her soft body against him. How long had it been since he'd last held a woman? Months, at least. Still, had any other felt so soft...?

Enough, Joseph, he chided himself. There's no time for this.

Moving to a tree stump, he sat her down and tried to assess the damage she'd endured.

Tears streaked from her eyes...eyes the color of doe's hide, he noted. Gently, he brushed dirt from her mouth, revealing lips of pale pink. Beneath the mask of dirt he saw patches of golden brown skin. It was as if the sun had kissed her gently to bring forth such a delicate color. Her hair was disheveled, but he could make out thick black waves as they met in a bun at the nape of her neck. She was beautiful.

"Tia." A little Hutu boy with tear-stained cheeks threw himself at the woman.

Amazed at the little boy's strength, Joseph stepped back to give him room. A woman, apparently the child's mother, moved forward to finish the doctoring task he'd begun.

Sensing the American was in good hands, Joseph turned away, only to be stopped by a warm hand on his wrist.

"*Merci*," the exotic woman said in French.

Apparently, she'd thought he hadn't heard her the first time. Inclining his head in acknowledgment, Joseph allowed himself a long indulgent look at the beautiful woman.

She smiled and released him.

The warmth of her fingers remained with him as he approached his men.

Leonard Bolongo, his second-in-command, stood coiling the rope used for the recent rescue. He looked up as Joseph approached. "What now, Commander?" he asked. "Kill them?"

Joseph surveyed the refugees. For the first time in two years, he'd forgotten to hate Hutus on sight. It was the American fogging his mind, he knew. "No," he told Leonard. "None are militia."

"Lucky for us," Leonard scoffed. "Or was it your plan to put us all in danger?"

He'd done just that with his impromptu rescue, but it wasn't Leonard's place to bring it up. "Don't challenge me, Bolongo."

"If you let them live, then warn them..." Leonard grunted as he slung the rope into a nearby pack. "To stay the hell out of my way."

Joseph turned a wary eye on the man. "How can your appetite for killing be so keen after so many battles, Leonard?"

Tugging the pack onto his back, Leonard smiled wickedly, revealing a missing front tooth. "Isn't yours, Commander?"

Joseph felt guilt weigh on his chest like a gestating elephant. In fact, he was weary of killing. It didn't seem to matter how many Hutus he killed, the guilt never diminished. That's why, each morning, he had to talk himself into a hate powerful enough to kill.

He was a successful warrior. Yet, what he did daily gave him no joy. Would things be different if he'd finished his schooling? There would still be this war. A diploma would of been useless against Hutu guns.

Shaking away personal thoughts, he looked at Leonard. "Gather the men. There are Hutu militia on the border of Rwanda. We'll tally our rations and decide our plan of attack," he ordered.

The squat man frowned as he replied, "Fantastique." He moved out to complete the assignment.

"The rest of you, set up camp." Joseph's men scampered to obey. It was too late to continue today. It would be dark soon, and the path even more treacherous.

Joseph's head ached. The Zairian Hutu army followed only a day or two behind. So far, their preparation and stealth had given them the upper hand in the war. Now wasn't the time to lose that advantage.

Joseph scanned the sober, weary faces gathered around a large fire. He should tell them the light made them easy prey. But why bother? It shouldn't matter to him if they died at the hands of another rebel unit.

A heavy sigh eased passed his lips as he watched the large gathering of Hutus. They shared their meager rations of food and water. The children played despite their long journey that day. A woman with plump, shiny cheeks rocked the baby in her arms to sleep. Even as a young boy, he remembered his mother holding him that same way. How safe he'd felt. How soothing the song she sang to him.

The American woman, Tia, lay on her side telling a story to the children gathered around her. Occasionally, a wrong move caused her to grimace, but the children remained enraptured by her tale.

Joseph stared longingly. It was this, he missed most. The feeling that all could be endured, overcome, within the loving arms of family.

Several of the men rose from their place at the fire and walked toward his camp. On guard, Joseph sprang to his feet, his hand went instinctively to the gun at his waist. His men were on their feet in seconds.

"Please, we come in peace," the man who led the others held up his hands. "Do not shoot." He had the precise diction of a scholar.

Joseph thought the man looked familiar. "What do you want?"

"My name is Fidele Zavi. I wish to talk with you, sir." A warm smile could be discerned in the faint light.

Joseph could see the man was unarmed and relaxed. "What about?" he asked.

Zavi stepped closer to Joseph and extended a hand. "Men talk more comfortably if they know each other's names, wouldn't you agree?"

Joseph studied the man skeptically. "My name is Joseph Desiré. I don't believe enemies can talk comfortably at all."

Zavi lifted one elfin eyebrow, shrugged and dropped his hand to his side. "If you insist. We came to ask your benevolence, Mr. Desiré."

"My benevolence?"

"We ask that you spare our lives so that we can return to our homes in Rwanda."

"And in return?" Joseph crossed his arms, amused by the man's gutsiness.

"We will share all that we have." He opened up his arms in generosity.

Joseph could tell they didn't have much, but in fact, they had more than he and his men. It had been a long time since they'd found a stocked aid shelter to replenish their supplies. Besides, the man may be his enemy, but he could almost hear his mother warning him against disrespecting another man's gifts. Before he could accept the deal, Leonard stepped forward.

"We don't need anything from you dirty Tutsi dogs!" Leonard nearly spat his disapproval.

"Fall back, Bolongo!" Joseph held close to his temper before turning back to Zavi. "In truth, we won't make it to Kigali with what we have. We will happily take whatever you offer. But you must know, we are headed to fight the Hutu militia at the border. You follow at your own peril."

Leonard mumbled something as he strode angrily away.

Fidele gave a humble bow of his head. "*Merci*, Monsieur Desiré." He retreated to his camp, the other men nodding and pounding their enthusiastic approval upon his thin back and shoulders.

Joseph's men stood around with wonder written all over their faces. "Couldn't we just kill them and take their food?" David, a young rebel asked innocently.

"We're low on bullets as well." It was the truth. "It is best if we save them for armed enemies."

His reasoning seemed to meet with their approval, with the exception of Leonard who nearly threw himself upon his sleeping bag.

Joseph had to remain wary. His second-in-command would rather kill than look at the Hutus. For some unexplainable reason, Joseph didn't want any of these people harmed. Perhaps it was because, for the first time, a Hutu had looked him directly in the eye and spoken to him with respect and asked for mercy.

And then, there was the American. His eyes drifted to her. A pulling in his loins accompanied his gaze. She was so soft and weak. He doubted she was physically able to endure the upcoming days of their journey. Yet, he couldn't make concessions just for her or they would all starve. She'd have to make it, or be left behind.

Tia lay motionless and stared at the lone star beyond the tree limbs. Now that it was night, she could no longer steal looks at the man who'd saved her life.

He'd ordered about his men with precise commands and not a little bit of bad temper all afternoon. Where had he come from, she wondered?

She'd watched sweat glisten on his smooth, dark skin as he'd set up tents alongside his men. His uniform, torn and minus a few essential buttons, revealed wide plates of chest muscles. Muscles that bunched wonderfully whenever he struck a tent stake with his hammer. How odd that he worked as hard as his men. Clearly, he was in command, but why didn't he just supervise, like other ranking officers? Maybe his army wasn't like the American army.

And why was he so serious all the time? Actually, Tia thought, his countenance bordered on grim. Yet, his ever present frown only added to the ebony perfection of his face. High cheekbones and a square jaw were features God had chiseled with bold strokes, making him the single most attractive man she'd ever set eyes on.

But boy, did she know how deceiving looks could be. Mason was a handsome man who turned his share of female heads, though he hadn't given any of them a second glance until the last year of their marriage. She should have seen it coming. They were fighting all the time. He started coming home late. Still, she hadn't expected him to chase supermodel Cynthia like a dog after a bone. If there was any justice in the world, having their baby had made Cynthia fat and saggy.

Sighing, Tia tried to shift from her back to her side without any luck. Her myriad scrapes burned in agony despite Sarini's cleansing with water and hydrogen peroxide from their medical emergency kit. This evening, she'd even forced off her boots to tend to the open sores on her feet. There was no way she would survive another day in shoes.

Surveying her arms, thighs and midriff, Tia concluded that there was barely a square inch of her that wasn't bound. "I look like a mummy," she said to no one in particular.

"What's a mummy?" Denis stirred somewhere near her head.

"A dead person wrapped up in bandages," she supplied.

"Oh." Denis came around to sit by her side so she could see him. "But, you not dead," he said in all his three-year-old wisdom.

"True." Tia struggled against pain to lift her pointing finger. "But I wish I were."

Of course, her sarcasm was lost on the child. She smiled at his frown of contemplation.

Fidele approached the small fire of their family camp and took Denis in his lap. He and the other men had been talking with their visitors.

With a sudden thrill, Tia struggled to roll onto her side. "Who is that guy and what's his story?" Tia wanted to know everything she could about the man who'd saved her.

Fidele's narrow features looked solemn in the flickering firelight. "This man is Joseph Desiré. He's a Tutsi rebel."

Tia sucked in her breath in unison with the rest of the Zavi clan. It was Tutsi bullets and mortars that had driven them into the jungle.

Sarini rose and began collecting their blankets. "We must leave."

"Wait." His thin fingers on her arm halted his wife's packing. "He's not going to harm us."

Alarmed at Fidele's trust in a Tutsi, Tia asked, "How do you know?"

"Because their enemy is the Zairian Hutu government, not us."

Tia frowned. "You told me yourself how the Tutsis slaughtered thousands of Hutu civilians in Rwanda a couple of years back. Not to mention those people in Uvira." Flashbacks of the slaughter played in Tia's mind.

Fidele nodded. "In retaliation, yes. We Hutus killed them first."

"Does it matter?" Tia argued. "The Tutsis are your enemies. This guy has guns and we have nothing. We could all be dead by morning."

"Did he not save you from death today?" Fidele lifted his pointed eyebrows in challenge.

"Yeah," Tia admitted. "But I'm an American. What about you?"

Sarini nodded vigorously. "Yes, Fidele. We must run."

Fidele lifted a hand to invoke silence. "I cannot explain it. I trust this man. If he wanted to kill us, he would've done so already."

Tia relaxed a little. "I can't argue with that. But why? Why isn't he trying to kill us?"

"That I do not know." Fidele's forehead wrinkled as he stared into the flames of their small fire. "He warns us that they are on their way to wage battle on the

Rwandan border with Hutu militiamen. He will provide us safe escort, if we wish. But we will be walking into battle."

Tia shifted uncomfortably. The last thing she wanted was to find herself in the middle of another battle. "What shall we do?"

Sarini gave a distressing cry. "We never find home."

Fidele gave her a sober look. "We will get home. I promise you."

"We follow him into war?" Sarini's voice broke on the last word.

Fidele nodded and silence fell on his clan. "Without him and his rations, we don't have enough food and fresh water to get us all the way home. And I don't think you can take much more walking." His eyes glinted fiercely in the firelight. "Desiré, his supplies and his soldiers are our only hope."

"What happens when we reach the Rwandan border and the fighting begins?" Tia asked.

"We will go around it," Fidele said with confidence. "Commander Desiré says he will travel toward Cyangugu. We will head north and reach Kigali only a few days later than we planned." He looked hopefully at his wife.

Sarini didn't answer, just sat down heavily on the matted grass. "A few days more." She buried her face in her hands.

The small fire crackled in its enclosure. If additional wood wasn't added soon, it would die. So too would they, if they didn't find a way to escape the war closing in around them. Tia prayed with all her heart that this plan would work. This time next week she wanted to be safely tucked away in her warm bed inside her DC apartment.

Sarini's quiet sobs were shared by two of her daughters who huddled tightly around her.

Denis drifted to sleep in his father's lap. Gently, Fidele laid him on his blanket and then moved to hold his weeping wife.

At least Sarini had Fidele and their children to cling to. Tia had no one.

And she didn't need anyone, she reminded herself. That's what this trip was all about—her helping other people and standing on her own and once again, she'd jumped impulsively into a situation and found herself drowning in her own incompetence.

She wasn't helping anyone. Fidele and Joseph Desiré were helping her.

Conversations around other fires soon stilled. Echoes of futility seemed to hang in the stagnant night air as the other families, no doubt, dwelled on this same dilemma. Is it possible to trust your enemy?

Tia sighed and shook her head. "None of this makes sense," she said. Rolling to her back, she stared again at the lone star. Real fear settled inside her heart, overcoming the dull ache of her muscles. Would they be leaving one battle only to find another? If so, how would she find her way out this place back home?

Where was her backpack?

Feeling around with sore arms, she suddenly realized it must've fallen down the mountain when she'd stumbled. Her heart beat in increasing panic. That dumb bag was the last thing from home that she owned. Suddenly, she wondered if her dream of getting home had slipped away with it.

Get a grip, Tia. It's only a backpack. Taking a deep, cleansing breath, she closed her eyes and tried to think soothing thoughts. Instead, she found herself looking into the dark, stormy eyes of the Tutsi rebel, Joseph Desiré.

In her dream, for it must be, she found herself in his arms as bombs and bullets whirled in a tornado of chaos around them. He spoke English with an accent in his deep as midnight voice.

His arms tightened about her, even as the chaos escalated. Dead men with exploded skulls sought her with their hollow eyes, but he protected her, shielded her from all harm.

And still, he spoke. Like a song, his words drifted to her ears and warmed her face, calmed her soul. She lifted hands to his face, feeling the heat of his spirit beneath his beautiful black skin. Then she closed her eyes and willed him to kiss her, to possess her...

Her eyes flew open to dark of the night.

Shaking her head, she tried to dispel the lingering effects of her dream. How could she imagine Joseph to be a soft, gentle lover? He was so serious all of the time. Even when he'd rescued her, he'd simply barked orders at her as if she were one of his men. Yet, he'd been gentle and encouraging as they'd walked up the mountain.

Nonsense. He was a Tutsi rebel. His people were the ones who'd brought this insane war from Rwanda to Zaire, retaliatory or not. Perhaps Desiré only wanted to lull the Hutus into trusting him in order to kill them later.

No, she wouldn't wake them—they needed to rest. It was up to her to watch over them tonight. She owed them at least that.

Tia gathered her sleeping blanket and cautiously moved down to where Joseph and his men were camped out, her heart beating wildly. Finding a large tree, she all but dove behind it, first checking for snakes with a long stick before sitting down. Fidele may have been teasing about the stick's usefulness in fending off snakes, but she could always use it as a weapon if necessary.

When her breathing calmed and her heart returned to a normal rhythm, she listened. Only grunts and the occasional snore could be heard behind her, but the sounds reached her ears clearly. If the soldiers moved, she'd be the first to know and warn her friends.

Three

Joseph watched the woman's slow progress down the path. Tiptoeing gingerly and cursing beneath her breath, she approached his camp. It was the American, he was sure of it.

Curiously, he charted her course until she disappeared behind a large tree on the opposite side of the clearing. Shrugging, he lay back down. Maybe she had to relieve herself.

Hands behind his head, Joseph watched and waited for her to reappear. After many long minutes, he decided he'd better check on her. It would be just like her to fall and hurt herself again. He'd seen many American tourists who could hike and climb the winding trails of the bush with the best of Africans—this wasn't one of them.

Joseph reached the tree, planted a hand against it and poked his head around to see what she was doing. It was her gentle snore that caught his attention.

Lowering himself to one knee, Joseph took a closer look. She sat with her back against the tree and a blanket draped around her shoulders. Her head had dropped to her left shoulder as she slept. "Tia," he whispered, remembering what the child had called her.

She moaned sweetly and rolled her head toward him. A narrow slice of moonlight lit her golden skin. Intrigued, Joseph touched her cheek. It was like the fine silk scarf his mother once had.

Holding his breath, he willed her to remain sleeping as he let his fingers drink of her softness. His hands trailed from her cheek to her neck and back again.

Tia remained asleep even as he felt an awakening in his blood. Just being near her sent warmth flooding into unsuspecting places—thawing emotions hidden in cold corners of his heart. He put a finger to her open lips, tempted by their pale perfection. Would she scream if he kissed her?

Removing his hand, Joseph re-adjusted her blanket around her shoulders. He was a soldier, a fighter, not a lover. As the blanket moved, her feet were exposed. Joseph frowned at the bandages, imagining how raw her blisters must be.

Why was she here? He'd wondered all day. Probably an American tourist who got lost from her group. It was obvious that hiking for many days was not something she was used to. He and his men had followed the group of Hutus from a parallel path throughout the afternoon. Joseph had noticed how tiring the journey had been on the foreign woman. It hadn't surprised him in the least that she'd stumbled off the narrow path and down the mountain.

He'd run like the wind to save her. Strange, he thought. He hadn't given her rescue a second thought. It seemed as if instinct alone had guided his movements and sent him down the mountain after her. His mother had often spoken about fate. About how some things needed to happen——some people needed to meet.

Was he somehow fated to meet this woman?

Insanity. He shook off the strange feeling that traveled up and down his spine like the stroke of familiar fingers.

Tia's mumbling regained his attention.

One golden arm moved from beneath the blanket, a large stick settled loosely in the palm of her hand.

Suddenly, Joseph was glad he hadn't attempted to steal that kiss. He grinned—an expression he'd had little practice at in the past two years. Soft and weak, hah.

He rose, but stared a while longer before walking away. By the time he reached his sleeping bag, he was smiling. "Tia," Joseph looked back at the tree, "I think I love you."

A shiver coursed through Tia's body, awakening her. She felt wet and cold. The heavy air had cooled without the sun's touch and penetrated her to the very marrow.

She peered into the mist surrounding her. The morning sun lit the fog, giving it a ghostly glow. Moving her aching body away from the tree, she vowed to build a fire to sleep by next time.

Rising to her feet was an ordeal. Stiffness invaded every muscle of her legs and back, while her feet screamed with pain. She wondered what time it was.

Carefully, she peered around the tree toward the Tutsi camp. The soldiers were all but packed for another day's journey.

"Damn." Alarmed, she looked up the path for signs of any living Hutus. To her relief, they were collecting belongings as they had each morning since this nightmare had begun.

Clutching her back and grimacing from a collage of aches, Tia managed to haul her blanket and herself back to the Zavis' small camp.

On her journey back up the path, she noted the curious glances of the Tutsis. An ugly, gap-toothed man gave her a leering grin.

Turning her head, she pretended not to notice the evil gleam in his eyes. Noticeably absent from the camp was Joseph. Obviously she was a poor lookout if he'd left and she'd slept right through it. So much for Tia the Protector.

She reached the Zavis' fire just as Fidele and Sarini surfaced from sleep. Tia sat down heavily.

"You're up already, my American friend?" Fidele questioned her with a wide yawn as he threw off the plastic tarp. Drops of moisture rolled from it in small streams.

"Yeah. I couldn't wait to start another day," she said wryly.

"Ah, and I don't blame you." Fidele searched the tree-tops for something. "Look there." He pointed to a patch of sky above the mist.

Tia watched a silhouetted bird fly by—nothing else. "Yeah, nice bird," she said without much enthusiasm.

"It's not the bird I want you to see. It's the Promise."

"The Promise?" She eyed Fidele warily. Was this another of his jokes?

"Absolutely. It's like I tell my children." Several of them looked in his direction. "If the sun comes up, you're promised another day. Only you can decide what's to be made of it."

Tia smiled and looked into her friend's eyes. "How profound, Fidele. And I thought you were only good for a few laughs."

Fidele rose and stretched into the morning air. "I'm good for a great many things. Ask Sarini."

His wife raised an eyebrow at his lurid tone. Lifting a corner of her mouth, she tried not to smile. Something warm and sweet crossed the space between them as they held each other's gaze.

A sprinkling of their warmth fell upon Tia. She looked away, a little embarrassed at witnessing the tender moment. And very envious at never having such a feeling pass between herself and Mason in their entire six years together.

Suddenly, all of her shortcomings fell upon her in one large bundle. If she'd been a better wife, Mason wouldn't have divorced her. If she'd been able to have a baby, he would still be with her.

If she were at home, now would be the time to hit the corner convenience store and buy some great binge food.

As it was, Tia didn't even have her backpack to dig through for her last few pieces of candy. Nor did she have a toothbrush, she realized, running her tongue across her gritty teeth. Or a hairbrush.

Pulling the ponytail holder from her hair, she let her curls fall en masse about her shoulders. The heavy curls were unruly enough when she did have the proper grooming tools, but taming them now with just her fingers was proving to be an impossible task.

Fidele's gaze moved to someone behind her. "Was there something you needed, my friend?"

Tia whirled around to see Joseph standing near a tree, holding what looked like sandals in his hand.

Without ceremony, the man handed the shoes to Tia. "Put these on. We'll be walking far today." He walked past her toward his camp.

"Gee, thanks," Tia spoke to his retreating backside. She looked with skepticism at the unfashionable shoes that had been made of old tires and jungle vines.

"I think the Tutsi likes you." Fidele cocked an eyebrow in wicked amusement.

"D'ya think?" Tia frowned at the odd looking shoes, holding them between reluctant fingertips. "I've been given better gifts from people I hate."

Fidele leaned in close and whispered. "The least you could do is try them on."

Tia frowned. "You've got to be kidding."

Sarini came to stand beside her husband. "Tia, your feet have swollen so much, you'll never get your own shoes back on."

That much was true. Just the thought of putting her boots on over her bandages made her wince. "All right," she sighed. It wasn't as if anyone she knew would be around to see her.

She slid her feet between the rubber and the straps of the vines and tied the remaining length around her ankles. Fidele helped her to her feet, and she took a practice walk around the campfire.

It was amazing. The straps didn't hit any of her blisters and felt quite comfortable when she walked. "Hey, these aren't half bad," she marveled.

"Good fit." Sarini observed with a grin.

"Like they were made for her." Fidele winked, then laughed.

Tia could feel a flush of heat crawling up her neck. It was ridiculous to think Joseph had made the sandals for her personally. But then again, would he just happen to have a pair around that were her size? And how did he know how much her feet hurt?

Staring after the Tutsi, she watched him walk toward his men. He had a long-legged stride that spared any extraneous movement. His arms moved precisely, his head didn't stray from side to side—his walk was as intense as his personality.

Fidele moved to stand beside Tia. "Still think he's the enemy?" His eyes twinkled with mischief.

Tia crossed her arms and frowned. "I'll withhold judgment for a while longer." Actually, she wasn't sure what to think about the Tutsi rebel. He didn't seem the type to give anyone a thoughtful gift. No, he needed to get all of these refugees to Kigali and he didn't want her to hold them up—that's what the sandals were about.

Sarini gave her husband a worried look. "He's a soldier, not a relief worker. I don't trust him either."

Tia was delighted that Sarini looked upon her work with such favor and that her friend had reservations about Joseph Desiré as well. "You should listen to us, Fidele," Tia said knowingly. "Women have a sixth sense about these things."

"A sixth sense?" he frowned.

She sighed and rolled her eyes at having to explain the whole thing. "Yeah. You know the five senses...sight, sound, touch, hearing and smell?"

"Yes?" He still frowned in confusion.

"Well, it's a sixth sense...it's a saying..." Tia struggled to find an explanation.

He shook his head. "You Americans are very different," Fidele said sagely.

"Forget it." Tia sighed and began to pack her things
inside her blanket.

As they moved down the mountain path to begin the
day's trek, Fidele took the opportunity to poke fun at her.
"Does your sixth sense give you super powers? Perhaps we
could fly instead of walk." He laughed.

Tia glanced back long enough to glare at him. "I said,
forget it."

"No, no, my American friend. I want to discuss this
further." His laugh followed her down the path as she
sought to put a few people between them. Once she was
out of sight, she allowed a grin to take hold. Darn that
Fidele. He'd nearly made her forget how much her muscles were screaming today.

Tia took care to watch her footing—no more falling
down mountains for her. Looking ahead, she noticed
Joseph. He was a full head taller than the rest of the men,
most of whom Tia—at five-foot-four—could look levelly in the eye.

The path widened as they reached an unusually flat
section of the mountain. Tia took the opportunity to
catch up with the handsome Tutsi soldier. Maybe she
could get some answers from him about what he intended
to do with them while he waged war.

She cleared her throat as she came alongside him. A
strange warmth began in the pit of her stomach just from

being near the intense man. "Thank you for the sandals."
She wiggled her toes delightedly. "They're very comfortable."

Joseph stared straight ahead. "We've got a long way to
go. I couldn't take the chance of you falling behind..." He
turned to look at her. "Or down another mountain."

Tia sighed in exasperation. "You're as bad as Fidele
with the jokes. Only you should try cracking a smile when
you do it."

"I wasn't joking." His face was sober as stone.

"My mistake."

As she'd suspected, he wanted to get from point "A" to
point "B" in the most efficient manner, which was just
fine with her. The sooner she got to a real city, the sooner she could return to DC and put the horrors of Zaire
behind her. "How long will it take us to reach the border?" she asked.

Joseph squinted his narrow eyes and assessed their sur-
roundings. "I'd say three days at our current pace."

"Good." Tia pushed hair away from her face. "I can't
wait to have a hot bath and a soft bed."

It could've been her imagination, but Joseph actually
looked amused. "And you think you'll find these things
in Rwanda?"

"You don't think I will?"

His entire face frowned in contemplation. "It depends
on what's left standing."

Tia felt her optimism fade. "I see."

Silence marked their steps for a while as she tried to broach the subject foremost in her mind. "Joseph?" It was the first time she'd spoken his name. It felt oddly erotic as it sailed from her tongue.

"Yes, Tia?"

He knew her name, she realized. A soft spin of giddiness filled her chest at the way it sounded on his deep-as-thunder voice. It took a moment for her to recall her train of thought. "I...I was wondering what you're going to do with us once we get there?"

His dark eyes narrowed to slits when he frowned. "What do you mean?"

She chuckled to make light of the situation. "I'm not real anxious to get caught in the middle of a war. That's why I left Uvira with Fidele and Sarini."

"Why were you in Uvira?" His question sounded more like a challenge than a question.

"I was working there—with the Feed the World Foundation."

If possible, his entire demeanor darkened. "You're a relief worker?"

Tia's defenses went up. "Do you have a problem with that?"

He spoke a few mumbled curses under his breath, which pretty much confirmed that he did.

"Why?"

Something resembling a grin raised one corner of his mouth. "You don't know?"

"How would I?"

Joseph watched her for a moment, turned back to the path and spoke. "In Rwanda, my home, the relief organizations sent money for workers to buy food and fresh water for the poor."

"Exactly." Tia exclaimed. "What's wrong with that?"

Joseph stopped dead in his tracks and turned the full power of his disgust on her.

"Those so-called relief workers took the money. They are very rich now, living in good, solid houses while the poor wander the streets begging."

Refusing to show fear, Tia planted her feet and crossed her arms to bear the brunt of his anger. "Well, they're the exception," Tia responded. "Without relief organizations, millions of Africans would've died of starvation and disease over the past two decades."

"Millions of people have died of starvation and disease," he corrected. For the first time, his deep voice rose to meet the escalating levels of his wrath. "The relief you people offer is too little, and too late."

Tia clenched her jaws and her fists, knowing a blow to his chin would hurt her more than him. "You'd prefer it if we gave up, went home and didn't bother to save the few we can?"

"Isn't home where you're going now?"

"Only because it's too dangerous to stay."

"The going gets tough and feeding the world turns into an inconvenience, doesn't it?"

"I'd say war is a bit more than an inconvenience," Tia countered. "If we die, we can't help."

Joseph straightened to his full height. His anger was spent. "You actually believe you make a difference?"

Tia knew her week of service had benefited the Hutus. She'd fed them, doctored them to the best of her ability and told them a few stories to make them smile. Most of all, she'd talked with the children. Their eyes had sparkled and smiles lit their faces when she spoke of America and for a while...they knew hope. "Yes," she replied.

Joseph stared at her for a moment with his dark, narrowed eyes. The deep furrows of his brows softened as he spoke. "Then, perhaps, you are the exception." He turned and continued down the path.

Tia watched him go, wondering what could've happened to make the man so cold and cynical. Joseph's men paraded past as she contemplated their leader. There wasn't a thing about him that she liked mentally. Yet her body reacted to him like a live flame in high wind. Shudders still ran up and down her spine from their heated exchange.

Forcing herself to look at the people streaming past, she waited for Fidele and his family. Grabbing hold of Denis's hand, she fell in step with the Zavis.

Denis tugged on her hand to get her attention. "He a mean man, huh?"

Realizing that everyone had witnessed their argument, Tia felt a little embarrassed. "I don't think he's mean,

Denis." She wasn't lying. "He's just got a lot on his mind."

"Oh." Denis accepted her explanation, then pulled in front of her and held up his arms.

Sighing, Tia picked him up. He wrapped his little legs around her waist and laid his head on her shoulder. "Tell me story about 'Merica," he said with a yawn.

It was the way they passed the long hours walking. She told him about her country, and he asked a thousand questions about what she said. From time to time the older Zavi children piped in to quiz her as well.

Three more days, she told herself when her body and stories were equally exhausted. I'll be closer to home in three days.

And she'd never see Denis again.

His small sigh in her ear tugged at her heart. Suddenly, she wasn't so anxious to leave.

Joseph stabbed angrily at the rations on his tin plate. His men were huddled in small circles. Hunched forward, they spoke in hushed tones between fits of laughter.

Occasionally he caught the word "American" and he knew his embarrassing outburst of anger toward Tia was the catalyst for their muffled merriment.

He gulped down a drink of water, wishing it were alcohol, and prepared to venture into the jungle for his nightly patrol.

Leonard broke away from his group and loped toward him. The smile he wore was too wide even for his otherwise large face.

"Sir?" Leonard hissed the word through the gap in his teeth.

"Bolongo."

"The men want to know if they should place a guard on the American mademoiselle." He stuck a pink tongue where his top front teeth should've been and continued smiling. "Your anger toward her is greater than it is for the Hutus."

Stifled laughter flittered around the camp.

Joseph recognized the comment for what it was; another criticism about his waning commitment toward war. Curled fists at his side, he forced himself to keep a level voice. He refused to have two embarrassing displays of temper today.

"A man's Second should know better than to ridicule his leader." Hopefully Leonard had sense to let the subject drop.

The smile slid from Leonard's face only to be replaced by an ugly sneer. "Just trying to have a little fun, Commander. That's all." The firelight gleamed like the flames of Hell in the short man's eyes.

Widening his stance, Joseph prepared to take their verbal sparring to a physical level. It wouldn't be the first time he'd had to beat respect into the ugly little man.

"Take your fun back to your own fire, Leonard. I'm not in the mood."

"No harm intended, Commander." The short man's words were forced through clenched jaws. Slowly, he turned and walked in his odd side-to-side gait over to a group of soldiers who'd pretended to be busy readjusting their tent stakes. "Hear that, fellas?" his voice was a touch too loud for a whisper. "Says he's not in the mood."

Their masked snickers drifted past Joseph's ears, increasing his irritability. "I'm off for a perimeter check," he announced, pulling a long-bladed panga from his supplies.

"Aye, Commander," various men responded.

The sharp blade of the big knife sliced through plants and vines in deadly strokes. Imagining each stalk to be Bolongo's neck, Joseph thrilled at the man's demise with each accurate swing.

There was no real protocol in their rebel army. Leonard Bolongo had emerged as his second-in-command through a succession of battles. He'd fought harder and longer than any of the other men. It seemed his appetite for slaughter grew with each kill.

At the time, Joseph had considered Leonard a fiercely efficient warrior, an asset to his small unit. Now, he wondered at the man's allegiance. Was it to the Tutsis and their struggle to rule Zaire? Or was it only to create corpses?

Joseph's anger lessened the more he hacked, until finally, a quietness took hold of his mind. Stopping, he listened to the night sounds. Chattering monkeys and hooting owls sent their conversations echoing through the trees. But now there was a new sound. One he hadn't heard in a while.

He followed the quiet rushing sound until it led him to its source. A tiny stream—a trickle really. Joseph bent to taste the water. It was fresh. They weren't far from the falls then. Good news since their water rations were low.

Not only that, but they would need the protection the loud roar of falling water provided. He'd spotted a Zairian soldier earlier in the day—a scout more than likely. No doubt the noisy refugees and their colorful garb had pinpointed their location.

Joseph reclined, making a pillow of the soft moss surrounding him. Knowing his enemy, it would only take a day for the man to return to his troop and lead it back. He'd been certain to route his entourage in figure-eights today, to make it harder to follow their tracks. He smiled. It was a simple maneuver but it had kept the disorganized Zairians baffled for a week once before.

Fatigue settled over his body. His muscles relaxed. The soothing trickle of the water over rocks quieted his thoughts until he recalled the altercation between himself and Tia earlier in the day.

He'd scowled, insulted and shouted at the American,
yet she hadn't backed down. He didn't know whether to
be irritated or impressed with her glaring defiance.

It was the feuding of these emotions that made him
snap at her. It must've been. Because there was no other
reason. He'd known days ago as he'd watched her with the
Hutus, the way she'd laughed with the man called Zavi,
kissed and held the children, that she wasn't like the others he'd seen. She truly loved the people of his Africa.

Most visitors only looked upon the people with pity.

Joseph hated pity. The sad clucking and cooing nois-
es. The tears shed on the poor before fast retreats to comfortable homes in Europe or America.

Tia would leave, as well.

Joseph sighed. Relief workers had come and gone
from Rwanda, Burundi and Zaire for years. He'd accepted their presence like so many pesky gnats. And though
he didn't believe they were as helpful as they wanted to be,
none had made his blood rush like this one.

And here, with the stars as witness to his revelation, he
knew why. He loved Tia.

She was meant for him. It was as clear as the water
rushing beside him. He wanted the American woman as
much as he wanted to avenge his family's murders.

Wants. Sighing, he rubbed at his aching temples.
They haunted him. For years, he'd buried his wants deep
within his heart in a grave covered by the force of his will
and sealed with anger.

But when Tia fell down the mountain, something had jarred the coffin, awakening sleeping skeletons of emotion. He'd panicked at the thought of losing her and leapt to save her.

Cursing his own insanity, Joseph struggled to find a soft patch of grass to lie on. How could he be afraid of losing someone he didn't know?

"Besides, Desiré, you have nothing to offer this woman who has everything." His voice was hard and biting against the heavy night air. He possessed weapons, a stolen tent, United Nations rations—and the empty space beside his sleeping bag. Tia's father would surely not approve of a union.

Soon the Tutsis would control Zaire, he reminded himself. Then it would be his turn to have money, a good home ... something to offer a wife. But by that time, Tia would be in America—enjoying a lifetime of hot baths and warm beds. Unless he stopped her.

Joseph put a hand to his chest to enjoy the sudden strong pounding of his heart, eased of its heavy burden. Tia would be his. He had but to find some way to impress her. Only holding her again in his arms could ease the sweet ache pulling inside him. Only having her for the rest of his life would ease the dark pit of loneliness that had been his constant companion for two years.

Tia sighed and let her eyes fly open. She couldn't sleep. If she were home, a hot cup of cocoa and a good book would've been the remedy for her insomnia. She wasn't sure what to do in a Zairian jungle in the middle of the night.

Rising to her feet, her blanket slid down her legs as she stretched. Soreness still accompanied her every movement, but it was less severe. She might survive this ordeal yet. The insistent weight of her bladder urged her to find privacy in the nearby foliage.

The search for a clear spot devoid of crawling insects was much easier in the daytime, she decided, pushing back plant after plant. Though the moon shone here and there through the latticed leaves of the eight-foot-tall plants, it did little to diminish the shadows beneath the large leaves. She had to bend nearly to the ground to detect the busy little movements of the small creatures living there.

A sound stopped her. Immobilized by the heat of eyes trained upon her, she whispered shakily into the darkness, "Who's there?"

Leaves rustled behind her. Fear made her gasp. She spun around to meet her aggressor. Only the swaying of a large leaf told of the stranger's departure.

Tia dropped to the ground and pushed herself into a particularly dense patch of bushes. If he could hide, so could she. Her heart beat hard against her ribcage while she waited, not daring to breathe.

Rustling came from her left this time. Tia felt around for a stick or rock—anything hard enough to cause damage. The stalker moved slowly at first, leaves swayed in his wake. Suddenly he charged Tia. She scooted back until she met with a tree trunk.

Holding up the stone she'd found, Tia prepared to smash it into his face. Suddenly, a large, black monkey emerged from the dark bush, screamed at her in an unearthly pitch, then scampered up the nearest tree. Tia dropped the stone and held a hand to her heart to keep it from bursting out of her chest. "Great," she said breathlessly. "Killer Cheetah." Relief settled on her slowly. It would be a while before her legs regained their strength.

Her wet legs, she realized in horror.

She shook her head, grateful Fidele had missed this embarrassing event. He would've thought of a thousand ways to tease her about her lack of bladder control.

Leaning her head against the tree trunk, she wondered what to do about cleaning herself. Their fresh water rations were low and they needed it to drink.

Of course, she hadn't had a bath in nearly a week. What was one more odor? No. She shook her head. The layers of grime and filth were intolerable even though she'd become accustomed to the pungent smell of unwashed bodies.

Frowning, she sat quietly. Bathing. Such a simple luxury. When she got back home, she vowed never to take it for granted again.

A faint trickling sound reached her ears like an audible oasis. It had to be her imagination. She'd wanted water so badly that her mind had created the illusion of its exis-

tence. Still, sitting there listening intently, she felt com-
pelled to find the origin of the sound.

Pushing her way through the bush, she emerged into a
small clearing where a small gurgling stream continued to
call out to her. She was so delighted to see the water that
she almost peed her pants again.

"Oh, if only I had my backpack," she said wistfully.
The bottle of liquid soap inside would've made her night.

Squatting beside the stream, she wondered how best to
do this. Sitting in the water was not an option, it wasn't
nearly wide enough. Maybe she could boil some of it
and—no. She wasn't very good at making fires despite
Sarini's repeated attempts to teach her.

Tia looked around her newfound haven. Only the
occasional rock, a log and the natural privacy afforded by
rows of head high bushes lining the stream could be seen.
Well then, nothing to do but strip and wash her clothes as
best as she could by hand. The night had already begun
to cool, she'd have to hurry.

It didn't take her long to rinse out her clothes and beat
them against rocks to remove most of the dirt and odor.
Then she washed herself.

The water was cool, but not cold as it slid in meager
streams through her fingers and down her body. It was
refreshing to feel the stickiness of dried sweat rinse away.

She'd even managed to find a pool large enough to
stick her head into and rinse out her hair. It was still tan-

gled from lack of a comb or brush, but at least it felt better.

When she'd finished, she put the wet clothes back on and pulled tangles from her hair with her fingers. The soaked clothes caught the chill in the cold air and made her shiver.

It was time to get back to camp and its fire before she turned into a popsicle. She gathered small dried sticks and vines to fortify the flames and help her clothes dry faster.

Hugging her meager collection to her chest, Tia stopped suddenly in her tracks. Quizzically, she scanned the area around her. Every grouping of bushes looked exactly the same. Damned if she wasn't lost.

"Oh no." Pushing back fear, Tia attempted to find the place she'd first encountered the stream. It was amazing, the lack of distinction up and down the small embankment. Great. What to do now? Scream for Fidele and wake the entire camp? She'd be safe, but embarrassed— nothing new there.

Frowning, she chewed her lip and tried again to find her point of entry from the bush. There had to be a way to re-trace her steps and save herself. Tears of frustration stung the back of her eyes and her lip trembled beneath her teeth. How was it possible for the entire thing to look the same from start to finish? How was it that she couldn't do this one simple thing?

She dropped her wood and sat down heavily on the log—which sprang to life beneath her.

Joseph awakened instantly at the attack. Quickly, he rolled to his side, throwing his assailant onto his back. He straddled the man and brought the knife from his waist high up over his head to strike.

The man screamed and struggled. Joseph pushed a hand into the soft flesh of his...breasts?

"Don't kill me, Joseph! Please!"

Stunned, Joseph squeezed his eyes closed then opened them again to ensure he wasn't still dreaming. "Tia?"

"Yes," she replied weakly.

Lowering his weapon, Joseph released her and moved to the ground beside her. "Why are you wet?" he asked, feeling the chill on his hand and between his legs where he'd held her. "Did you fall into the stream?"

"No." She sat up and adjusted her clothing. "I was washing my clothes...for all the good it did me." Sticks and grass now stuck to her damp attire from their tussle.

"Why did you attack me?" he asked, still not sure if he was awake.

"I didn't attack you. I thought you were a log."

"A log?"

"Yeah." She blew out air and pushed hair from her face. "I was gathering wood to put on the fire so I could dry my clothes when I got back to camp. All of a sudden

I realized..." She shrugged. "I was lost. I just wanted to sit down and—"

"And you sat on me," Joseph concluded.

"Not intentionally. I was about to have a good cry," Tia admitted sheepishly. "But since I found you, I guess that won't be necessary." She cut her eyes sideways at him as the moonlight spilled down the wavy locks of her hair. Her face, half in shadow, gave her exotic features added mystery.

Once again, his emotions rattled. It was as if she appeared from his dream where she'd sat beside a stream combing her fingers through her hair, a blissful look on her face, the reflection of her quiet soul. Such beauty had to have been sent by the gods. She was meant to be his. But not here, not like this.

"Would you like me to take you back to camp?" he offered.

"If you don't mind," she hugged herself and shivered, "would you to build me a fire?"

Her sweet, pleading look sent currents of desire pounding through his veins like the great falls. She'd never know how tempted he was to take her in his arms and warm her with the heat of his need. He swallowed hard and fought for control.

"I'm not sleepy," Tia explained. "I'd just as soon sit and talk for a while."

"Talk?"

"Unless you're tired," she amended.

Nothing in his body was close to exhaustion. With just a look, Tia seemed to charge every muscle.

Control yourself, Desiré. Don't scare her away. Joseph bent down to assemble the wood she'd dropped. "I'm surprised you're still speaking to me after our...discussion today."

Her laugh was light, shaky. "I could say the same."

"Yes," he acknowledged. A wave of embarrassment washed over him. He examined each piece of wood with unnecessary care to hide this newfound emotion.

"You're an interesting person, Joseph."

"Am I?" He looked up. Hope soared to the night sky within him. She was smiling, her head cocked to the side.

"Yes. It's like...," she paused thoughtfully. "You don't allow yourself to be anything but angry."

The accuracy of her insight sent panic up his spine like an arrow through his heart. She had no right to make him feel—vulnerable. He wouldn't allow it.

"I thought you were an aid worker, not a mind reader," he bit out.

"Right there." She rubbed her arms and nodded. "You've just proven my point."

"I'm not angry." Gritting his teeth, Joseph struck the wheel of his lighter with a vicious flick of his thumb. He lit the dried moss lying beneath the carefully criss-crossed wood pile and sat back, elbows resting on his knees.

The flames caught on a particularly dry bunch of twigs and flared higher. It wasn't too large of a fire. Not high enough to bring unwanted attention from enemy eyes. Thankfully, the blaze captured Tia's attention as she moved closer to it.

Tia leaned her head back, exposing her long golden neck, and sighed. It was a sound so purely feminine that it provoked everything male in Joseph's body.

Her wet blouse clung to full, rounded breasts with vicious disregard to his rising discomfort. His eyes traced the lacy patterns of her bra beneath the transparent material of her blouse. Allowing himself a long, lingering gaze, Joseph quickly let go of his anger.

Painful cravings forced him to drop his head and study the blades of grass at his feet. He couldn't look at her and keep his lust in check. Couldn't without trailing hungry kisses along the soft skin of her neck.

"Joseph?"

"What?" He tightened his hands into fists.

"I've been wondering..." She pulled her wet blouse out and away from her body.

Catching the movement, he dared a sideways glance. "Hmm?" Did she know what he was thinking now?

Her eyes were dark and serious across the flames. "What makes a man kill another?"

Joseph frowned. "This is what you want to talk about?"

Nodding, she shifted a little in the grass. "There must be a heckuva good reason for someone to do such a horrible thing."

So, it was her turn to judge him. "You're asking why I kill?"

Tia shrugged.

The Darkness drifted over him like a fog, bringing with it the stench of burned flesh. It was an odor that seared his nostrils now as it had the day he'd discovered his family's charred remains. His lips curled downward as he gave his answer, "Revenge."

Four

Tia shivered as a cool, misty breeze cut through the warm flames to deliver Joseph's words. "Revenge? For what?"

No emotion showed as he spoke into the flickering light of the fire. "My father, my mother..." he said bitterly, "my sisters and brothers."

"Oh," Tia said quietly. "Who killed them?"

A twisted frown formed on his face—the reflection of his tortured soul. "Habyarimana, the Hutu president of Rwanda, sent orders to his men to slaughter all the Tutsis they could find two years ago."

Her heart grew heavy as she reached out to share his sadness. "I'm sorry. I wish there was something I could do."

Irritation flashed on Joseph's face. He retrieved his long blade from a clump of grass and stood over her. "Unless you can raise the dead and change ashes to flesh, I don't think there's much to be done."

Stunned, Tia watched him hack angrily through the bushes. It took a moment to realize the meaning of his words. His family had died by fire.

Pain had been so clearly etched on his features, she could almost feel it. She'd wanted to close the distance between them and give him what comfort she could. All she'd been able to manage was a rote expression of sympathy. The polite kind she gave to acquaintances when they talked of personal tragedies.

His shield of anger had gone up so quickly, there'd been no time to repair the damage. He needed to be free of the barrier of loneliness he'd thrown up around himself. She hoped, one day, someone would be able to break through to help him.

Turning, she let the warmth of the fire penetrate her cold, wet backside. She thought of Joseph making leaves fly with his machete. Chuckling, she knew there'd be no trouble finding her way back to camp now.

By the time her clothes were dry, Tia felt the heaviness of sleep pulling at her eyelids. Dousing the remaining flames with water, she followed the path of tattered leaves back to the camp. The brief walk was enough to make her cold all over again.

Shivering, she lowered herself onto the thickest patch of grass she could find and threw her blanket over her legs.

Feeling his stare, she turned. Joseph sat outside his small tent a few yards away, knees up, arms around them. She faced him in the faint light of the stars, expecting to find the same dark anger as before. But not this time.

His presence warmed her inside like a hot chocolate and Peppermint Schnapps on a winter's day. Entranced, she felt the heat of desire flare inside her high as the flames he'd coaxed into being an hour ago.

He wanted her. Realizing this made her lose connection with the ground. Tia parted her lips, desperate for a normal breath. She stared back at his silhouette——helpless to do anything more.

Joseph dropped his head suddenly, breaking their connection.

Tia felt an abrupt reconnection with the earth. The spell had been broken. She watched him in dazed confusion.

Joseph's shoulders lifted twice as if he were taking deep breaths. Then, without looking up again, he rolled to his knees and crawled inside his domed, one-person shelter.

Tia lay down and stared at the sky in disturbed contemplation. In that flash of a moment, her emotions had flown higher than they ever had. Even now, she was weak, dazed, lightheaded and giddy all at once.

What was it about the joyless Tutsi warrior that could make her feel a path of fire race through her veins?

Purpose.

It was his singular intensity of purpose she was drawn to. He never doubted what he would do next. Whereas her whole life was a series of "what nows?"

She'd gone to college, because it was expected of the daughter of a senator and a nationally-acclaimed columnist. She'd married Mason because he was the most eligible of all the bachelors at Howard University and all the other girls were falling all over him.

And last, she'd allowed Mason to dismiss her and their marriage with a river of tears but not much of a fight. She'd run to Zaire to escape him and her misery.

Tia rolled onto her side, pulled the blanket over her shoulders. Zaire was its own misery and now she was running from it. Couldn't wait to find an embassy, a plane and get out. Except now...

She lifted herself onto an elbow and looked over the dark forms of refugees and rebels lying on a grassy clearing. Eventually, she let her gaze rest on Joseph's tent. Her body glowed warmly.

Now she wasn't in such a hurry to return to America. Joseph had been waiting for her to return to camp safely. Had all but invited her over to his camp with his smoky stare. But she hadn't done it.

"Coward," she whispered to the wind. What would happen if for once, she fought for what she wanted? Would the cold fear that lived inside her finally go away? Who was she kidding? She could no more fight than Joseph could break down in a fit of laughter.

Joseph awoke from a disturbed sleep and crawled outside his tent. He stood, smelled the wet air, and listened. An abnormal silence pervaded the lush greenery around them and the scent of danger mingled with the morning mist. His body hummed with foreboding. There would be death today.

Quickly, he awakened his men and signaled them to stay silent. It took less than a half hour for them to arouse the Hutus, pack supplies and start walking.

Joseph steered clear of the Zavi family. Last night he'd waited, what seemed an eternity, for her to emerge from the bush. Just when he'd thought he'd have to go after her, she'd appeared.

Images of the woman had whispered their way inside his dreams like so many sweet promises. The sound of her laughter and light in her smile had kept The Darkness at bay for the first time in years.

Yet, she'd taken what was familiar and replaced it with crashing waves of violent desire. The damned woman had made him awaken earlier during the night to a wet bedroll. He couldn't afford to be further distracted if a battle was coming.

Leonard came abreast of Joseph and matched his stride. "Do you feel it, Commander?"

Deepening his frown, Joseph nodded, knowing the man smelled war on the air as well.

"What're we gonna do about the Hutus?" He said it nastily. He'd just as soon kill them, Joseph knew. Another, like Habyarimana, who thought very little of innocent human lives.

"We'll leave them at the falls." Joseph could hear the rush of water growing nearer.

"The sound of the water will hide the cries of their screamin' babies and cryin' women." Leonard followed his reasoning. "Then what?"

"Then we spread out to find Mobutu's soldiers."

Leonard shook his large, oblong head. "I say we stay put, and when the army finds us, we rip their guts out," he said with a wide grin.

Impatience bunched in Joseph's muscles. "When you get your own command, you can plan the strategy." He turned on Leonard. "I won't lose more of my men because of your stupidity. We'll do as we've always done—trap them and kill them one by one. Understood?"

"Whatever you say, Commander." Leonard's face scrunched in distaste. "We'll run like cowards."

Joseph ground his teeth at the man's insolent tone. "Another word, Bolongo, and it won't be Zairian gunfire you'll need to fear."

Joseph lengthened his stride, leaving Leonard to his cursing. He would deal with him later.

Around noon, the mist which had artificially darkened the sky gave way to the first rays of sunlight. They'd nearly reached the falls. The sound of crashing water would soon make it difficult to speak and be heard. He ordered his men to leave a few spare weapons with the refugees.

On impulse, Joseph walked up to Zavi and thrust a rifle at him. "Take this."

Fidele accepted the weapon uneasily. "I don't know how to use this," he cradled the gun like a fragile baby.

"Watch." Joseph showed him how to release the safety, load the magazine of bullets, and use the sight to target the enemy. "Can you do it?"

Fidele's adam's apple bobbed in his throat as he nodded his head in reply.

Joseph then turned to Tia and thrust a gun at her. "You too."

Tia made no move to accept the weapon. "What for?"

"Wise men prepare for the unexpected." He pressed the butt of the gun into her palm.

"Wise men don't put guns in the hands of women who don't have a clue how to use them." She grasped it to keep it from falling. "I've only shot my father's skeet rifle before. I don't know how to use a gun."

"You're right." Joseph stopped and scanned the area. "I'd better give you a quick lesson."

Ignoring her continued protests, Joseph set up targets using dead chimpanzee skulls atop long sticks. From the number of bones, he guessed disease had taken the primates rather suddenly.

"This is sick." Tia crossed her arms, frowning at the macabre targets. The gun dangled from her finger toward the ground.

"Raise that up before you shoot your foot." Joseph ordered, moving to her side and holding back a smile.

Quickly, Tia complied, holding the gun high and away from herself.

His men and the surrounding Hutus gave wide berth to the woman and the weapon.

"Smart." Joseph acknowledged their obvious distrust, grabbed the gun, turned the safety on and handed it back. "Now it won't go off unless you want it to."

Skepticism covered Tia's face. "You're sure?"

"Quite." Joseph moved behind her. "Hold it up and point at the skull on the right."

Tia grabbed the butt with both hands and did as instructed.

Joseph glided his palms the length of her arms, feeling for tension. He met with an unexpected reaction himself.

Tia gave a small cry of surprise.

"I didn't mean to alarm you." He spoke softly in her ear, suddenly enjoying his student more than he'd planned.

Tia didn't answer. Nor did she step away.

Joseph decided that was a good sign. "Now. Hold your arms steady. Elbows straight. Plant your legs firmly and I'll brace you for the recoil."

Tia widened her stance.

Joseph pressed his thighs behind hers and held her hips gently.

"How's this?" she asked, her voice a bit husky.

His hands traveled up and over sweet curves to her waist, then up to her extended arms. "Perfect," he murmured.

"I meant my aim," Tia scolded without much venom.

Joseph moved aside the silky strands of her wayward hair to check. "Looks good," he said sincerely. "Switch off the safety and take a shot."

Tia did as she was told, replanted her feet and took aim. Steadying the weapon, she pulled the trigger and sent the monkey skull into a spin. The recoil pushed her against Joseph.

"Excellent." Joseph held her tight, enjoying the warm smell of her skin and the way she molded perfectly within his arms.

Tia's breasts rose and fell rapidly with her excitement. "That was good, huh?"

He'd like to tell her how good, but was afraid it would come out wrong.

"Once more." A bit reluctantly, Joseph helped Tia to her feet to try again. Maybe her first shot was pure luck. "This time try to keep your feet under you."

Her second shot caught the skull squarely between its vacant eye sockets and sent it sailing into the brush.

"Did you see that?" Tia turned into his arms. "I actually hit it."

"Remarkable." Joseph reveled in her enthusiasm. He couldn't imagine wanting anyone more. If not for spectators, he would've taken her right then and there. "You're a natural."

Joseph's men moved to inspect the monkey skull. Tia, immensely pleased with herself, ran over to take a look as well. Bolongo hung back—the scowl on his face evidence of his displeasure.

"Good shot, hey, Leonard?" Joseph decided to rub it in. "I think she's better than you are with that gun."

Predictably, his teasing brought a rash of cursing from his second. "Put a knife in her hands and we'll see how she does," he threatened.

"A few more practice shots and we'll be on our way," he announced to Tia. "And how about you, my friend?" He looked at Fidele who stood with the machine gun away from his body. "Would you like to take a few shots?"

"I—I—," Fidele shook all over. "Well, no. No, I'll be fine." He sat the weapon down gently and took two steps back from it.

Joseph smiled at the man and thought about taking the machine gun back. Clearly Zavi was more afraid of the gun than he was the enemy. But, Tia. For a woman loathe to touch a weapon, she'd proved to be a better marksman than any of his recruits. She'd adjusted quickly to the gun's recoil, taking away his excuse to support her.

Just as well.

Each touch only served to increase his desire. When she'd completed a round, he tossed her targets back into the pile of bones. "I feel sorry for any man who crosses you." He put a finger through a clean bullet hole in a skull. "He won't survive if you can shoot a man as cleanly as these ape bones."

"I still don't believe in using these things for anything other than recreation." She turned the gun over in her hand and switched the safety back on.

"Suit yourself." Joseph turned up the path, proudly walking beside Tia. He didn't expect she'd really have to use the gun, but the impromptu lesson made him feel better about leaving her.

Tia walked alongside, struggling to find a home for her new possession. Finally, she shoved it inside her blanket along with her food dish.

"If you need that, you won't be able to get to it fast enough," Joseph said.

"If you do your job," Tia eyed him levelly, "I won't need it. What am I saying?" She shook her head in disbelief. "Why do you have to kill these people?"

"To keep them from killing us." Joseph stared straight ahead.

"It's just that simple for you, isn't it?" Tia couldn't help feeling disappointed. How could anyone be so calloused about killing? Especially one she'd grown so fond of?

Tia could tell her question angered him because of his tensing jaws. He didn't bother to answer. Instead, his pace quickened and he began barking orders to his men. He shouted over the rushing water, able to get the Hutu men to understand that they were to stay put with their families until he and his unit returned. He ignored Tia, making her feel bad.

She refused to let him see how hurt she was. Corralling the children, she proceeded to find a halfway quiet place to sit and tell them stories.

Fidele found her and told her to follow him. He wanted to watch the battle.

Silently, Joseph signaled his men. He didn't dare look back at Tia. If he did, she would see the wound she had sliced with her words. Nothing was simple here. She didn't understand.

Joseph found a path that led to a clearing. The Zairian soldiers would be coming this way. He was certain of it. He sent groups of four men in different directions to take cover in the foliage surrounding the opening.

The younger of the rebels accompanied him. Perhaps he felt a paternal need to keep the few teenagers at his side. They were the same age as his lost brothers.

Tucked discreetly behind tall plants, Joseph cautioned his men to remain as still as possible. The hardest part was the waiting. Anticipation tensed his muscles, the humidity making the bush hotter than usual. Sweat trickled down his back and face. Joseph wanted desperately to scratch the sudden itches that had sprung up all over his body.

Careless footsteps and casual laughter took his mind away from his discomfort. Zairian soldiers approached the clearing. Bits and pieces of their conversation reached his ears. They spoke of the village they'd just raided, amused by the screaming of the women as they'd used their bodies. Bragged about shooting down unarmed men.

Joseph's stomach turned. How had killing innocent people become so rote to them, to himself? Hadn't he ordered the raid on Uvira though they had no evidence of the militia being present? Hadn't he intended to kill the Hutus he now escorted?

The laughter of the Zairians echoed like the ghosts of his past in Joseph's ears. "We all deserve to die," he said angrily. He moved his automatic rifle from his shoulder to his hands. He heard his men release panting breaths of apprehension as they raised their own weapons.

A strange hollowness pushed aside fear and anxiety within Joseph and, as it had from the beginning, The Darkness filled him—numbing his senses. There would be many details of this battle he wouldn't remember. If he survived.

Tia held the tree limbs in a death grip and took a glance below her. The ground looked much too far away. Leaning her head against the trunk, she tried to slow the spinning in her head. "What in God's green earth was I thinking?" she asked the ragged bark.

"Tia." Denis giggled from somewhere above her. "Come on," he urged her.

Since she wasn't feeling too safe from this height, she worried about the three-year-old so high in the tree. Yet, it hadn't bothered Fidele or Sarini in the least to see their son scale the huge tree.

Fidele and two of his older sons were sitting high in the tree opposite them, long drapes of moss cushioning their seats. Even with a significant head start, Tia hadn't been able to climb the tree as fast.

A black monkey with wide eyes stared at her with undisguised haughtiness from a limb just beneath Fidele. She was almost sure it was the same one that had screamed at her the night before.

Tia scowled at the beast and renewed her efforts to scale the tree. Her grunting, groaning progress was jeered by the monkey in a loud screeching tone. He bounced up and down on his branch as if hoping for her to fall. She should've hit the darn thing with the rock when she'd had the chance.

It was an uncharitable thought, one she was sure wildlife preservation societies would frown upon, but it brought a smile to her face.

Tia pulled herself up one last time and swung her leg over a fairly wide limb. She smiled at Denis, wiped the sweat from her forehead and wrapped her thighs so tightly around the branch they hurt. "I made it."

"Oui." Denis smiled adoringly from a neighboring limb. "Look." He pointed his slender arm. "Soldiers."

Tia followed his small finger, fighting the urge to lie down and hug the branch she sat on. From their high vantage point, they could easily see the Zairian soldiers in their neat uniforms walking in the clearing at the bottom of the mountain—and the brief blaze of light as guns went off from the edge of the bush.

A sick feeling knotted in her stomach as several soldiers fell to the ground. Some obviously screamed as they died, though the sounds couldn't reach her ears over the rushing cascade of the falls.

Her queasiness escalated as the Tutsis raced in to finish off the Zairians in hand-to-hand combat. One rebel soldier slashed viciously, with a knife that glinted in the now unfettered sunlight. The way he slashed from one man to another seemed to make him ecstatic, as if he were playing instead of killing. The odd shape of his head gave away his identity. It was Bolongo, Joseph's second-in-command.

She shuddered in horror as he slit his next victim from stomach to chest. Blood spread dark against the man's uniform as he fell between the tall grasses.

Quickly, she looked over at Denis. He shouldn't be watching this.

The boy stared unblinking at the clearing. His mouth hung slightly open.

"You wanna get down now?" she asked him.

Shaking his small head, he continued to watch the men in uniforms.

Helplessly, Tia looked over at Fidele. Maybe he could talk the boy into leaving. "Fidele."

The thin man fixed an identical stare on the battle. He hadn't heard her.

"Fidele," she shouted over the roaring falls.

He turned and questioned her with his glance.

Tia pointed to Denis. "He shouldn't watch."

The man regarded his son gravely for a moment before answering her. "He must."

Stunned, Tia tried to understand what made him think war was something a child should witness. She herself was having a difficult time watching men die.

A sudden urgency sent her attention back to the battlefield. What about Joseph? Had he survived?

It took her only a moment to find him. He stood alone at the bottom of the hill. His shoulders straight, his head held level and steady. Blood stained the long blade that arched from his hand to his feet where several Zairian soldiers lay motionless.

The world went quiet around Tia as she stared at Joseph. He made no move as another Zairian fled the massacre in the clearing and ran downhill toward him. The Zairian's eyes widened as he nearly stumbled over the first body of one of his comrades and stopped within a few feet of the motionless Joseph. The man pulled his gun from his holster with shaking hands.

Joseph raised his bloody blade as if to deflect the bullets.

"What the hell are you thinking, Joseph?" She clung desperately to the branch beneath her. "He's got a gun."

An exchange of words passed between the men. The newly angered Zairian soldier put two hands to his gun and took aim.

"Oh," Tia wailed. She watched, but didn't want to. A man was about to die and she was scared beyond reason that it would be Joseph.

With one swift thrust upward, Joseph disarmed the man. His panga sent the gun flying into the bush. On the downward stroke, Joseph sliced the man from shoulder to thigh. Once again he stood still with the panga hanging from his side to the ground.

Geysers of crimson liquid spewed from the opening in the soldier's gut. Horrified, the man watched his life rush through his fingers. It took only seconds for him to sink to the ground beside another of his fallen brethren.

A hard convulsion hit Tia's stomach. Joseph had killed the man. Many men, she corrected herself. It would be impossible to disassociate the man with the deed.

The bitter taste of bile stung her throat and tongue. This wasn't a celluloid interpretation of war like she'd watched at the theater. Real men lay still on the ground. Men who would never rise to act this scene again.

Her thighs shook as they tried to keep her upright on the tree limb. Deciding she'd better get down, Tia swung her leg free of her perch and mostly slid her way back to the ground.

Sarini stood by looking concerned. "Are you all right?"

Unable to answer, Tia raced on scratched and wobbly legs to the nearest bush. In retching contractions, her stomach rid itself of its meager rations. All of her strength seemed to leave as well. Tia took a few steps back and sank to the ground. She lowered her head to rest on her knees and waited for the last echoing convulsions to stop wrenching her insides.

"Are you all right?" Sarini asked again, placing a hand on Tia's back.

"No," Tia answered honestly.

Worry creased Sarini's lovely face. "Who is winning?"

It struck Tia as an odd question. "Can there possibly be a winner?" she asked quietly.

Sarini didn't speak, only slid to the ground next to Tia. For a moment, the two of them sat quietly, lost in their own thoughts.

"Joseph and his men," Tia replied after a while. "They took the Zairians by surprise."

The Hutu woman's shoulders sagged. "What if they attack us next?" Sarini's fear of Joseph had compounded.

Tia knew they were in no danger from him, though she couldn't explain it. The man who'd just killed a half-dozen Zairians without blinking certainly was someone to be concerned about. But he'd softened toward the Hutus somehow. Maybe it was the way he smiled when he watched their children play—if he thought no one was looking. Maybe it was his thrusting the gun into Fidele's arms. Somehow she just knew. "I'm sure he would've killed us already if we were his targets." She took the woman's frail hands and rubbed warmth into them.

"Don't worry. He'll get us to Rwanda safely." Tia said with assurance.

Small footsteps sounded from behind Sarini. Denis whipped past his mother's skirt to Tia. "Y'okay?" He breathed heavily from his run.

Opening her arms to the child, Tia lowered her legs and held him in her lap. "I'm fine, Denis. How're you?" She still worried that watching the killing would leave a permanent scar on his small psyche.

"'Kay," he replied and settled into a more comfortable position. "Tell me 'bout 'Merica." He let out a big yawn.

Tia laughed at herself. This afternoon, he'd dream about whatever story she told him. Tonight, nightmares of the battle would be reserved for her.

Five

Joseph did not return to camp with his men. Bolongo would be leading a celebration with bootlegged whiskey by now. Instead, he jogged downstream alone, hoping to rid the chills in his blood with sweat. He half-listened to the bush as he wandered the bank of the small river until he reached a wide mountain valley, vaguely aware that he could be killed at any moment. He welcomed the thought.

Tall grasses swayed in the warm wind and the drunken laughter of hyenas echoed from a distance. Only blood, flowing like wine, from the jugular of some poor beast could so intoxicate them. He felt kin to the scavengers suddenly.

He'd lost no men today. Even Bolongo had forgotten their earlier disagreement, happy to have the stain of blood on his blade. By all counts, he'd led another successful mission. Why then, couldn't Joseph find peace?

Abruptly, he stopped his jog and dropped to the ground. He'd thought the only way to ease the nagging guilt within him was to exterminate all Hutu vermin who'd participated in the slaughter of a half a million Tutsis two years ago. The death of Rwanda's Hutu president had spurred the killings. But the Hutu barbarians had taken vengeance upon innocent civilians—his sisters and brothers among them. Ethnic cleansing. Again the horrible term quoted in a Rwandan newspaper flashed through his mind. President Habyarimana had ordered the killing. Laurent Kabila had later killed the Rwandan president. Shot down his plane. His stomach tightened at the horrid images of charred bodies littering the ground of his neighborhood or hanging from crosses. that still burned in his brain.

President Mboto Sese Seko advocated the same kind of slaughter here in Zaire, first prostituting precious African land and resources to other countries for personal gain, then supporting mass murder to keep anyone from contending his wealth and position. Joseph was happy to cross the border to fight, his quest was now to cleanse the land of ruthless dictators and those who followed him.

He'd prayed that, one day, he'd kill enough to ease his personal grief. But the anguish still burned in his heart. Joseph scanned the plain a second time. A slight breeze rustled the nearby brush. The day would have been peaceful, beautiful if not for the ugly scenes playing in his head.

He sighed knowing he wouldn't find the solace he so desperately needed, no matter how far he chose to run. Irritation made him tense and hot. Laying aside his weapons, Joseph stripped off his boots and dove into the river—its cool womb startling his hot skin. In moments, he grew accustomed to the temperature and submerged himself completely.

Resurfacing, he watched as blood fled from his uniform, seeping out on the fingers of small wavelets. He recalled an image from the Bible one of the visiting European missionaries had told him about. A man called Moses, putting his wooden staff to water as the power of his god changed the river to blood. A warning to the evil Pharaoh.

Joseph watched the blood disperse so far it could not be seen. God's magic worked the opposite way as well. Hadn't the missionary talked about baptism by water making you clean? He preferred that passage to the other. Closing his eyes, Joseph let the water push past him on its urgent journey to the lake several miles away, willing it to cleanse his mind and soul of the shadows of dead soldiers that haunted him.

It wouldn't be long before he followed them down the twisted path of death—only good fortune and a keen sense of strategy had prolonged his life thus far. Yet, death wasn't too good for him. He longed for it. To see his mother again. His family.

But then, what of Tia?

The thought of the woman sent a flood of lust to his loins. That and a gripping turn of his stomach served as a cruel reminder that he was still among the living. His hunger for the touch of Tia's creamy brown skin and soft curves was equal to his need for food, pushing thoughts of death far to the back of his brain.

Shadows of the bush lengthened as the light of the sun hung low in the sky. He should be securing the perimeters of their camp now—a task he trusted to no one save himself. A movement downstream caught his eye as he pulled on his boots. A cape buffalo, his long horns sweeping down, then up, watched him warily with one large, dark eye. After a moment, the beast returned to its drinking, its small ears pointed and alert, its breathing labored.

The red, raw flesh on its neck and hindquarters told Joseph why it was separated from its herd. Wild dogs had attempted to make a meal of him.

Severely handicapped by its wound, the injured cape buffalo would be dead by morning. No need wasting the rare opportunity for fresh meat.

Joseph glanced toward the foliage behind the beast, aware that any would-be carnivore could be lurking. "Better luck next time, friend," he said to his unknown competitor.

A hand on the hilt of his panga, Joseph turned his attention to the injured buffalo. Eyeing the beast steadily, he moved cautiously in its direction.

The horned beast pulled its nuzzle from the water and ran downstream a ways. Its reluctance to run further a clear indication of a fatal wound.

Joseph slowed his pace. He moved the big knife to his side and stood erect. Perhaps, if he moved slowly, the animal wouldn't be quite so suspicious of his real intentions.

This time when he advanced, the beast seemed less leery. It went back to drinking and ignored Joseph altogether.

Swiftly, Joseph raised the huge blade of his panga, prepared to deliver a swift, painless blow.

"Haven't you done enough killing for one day?" The woman's voice startled both man and beast, sending the latter hobbling into the scant cover of brush.

Joseph glared at the woman across the river. Tia stood with her legs wide set and arms crossed. Heated daggers of judgment flew from her stormy brown eyes, making him instantly angry and lustful.

No time to deal with her now.

Joseph tore into the bush in search of the animal, only to find its original predator standing guard over its inert form.

The hyena bared sharp, blood-stained teeth and growled a warning. Joseph hesitated only a moment. Unsheathing his gun, he took aim as the dog yipped and circled for attack.

Joseph's bullet ripped through mangy fur at the hyena's throat, dropping the creature in a heap at his boots.

Tia's voice carried through the bush to his ears. "You didn't kill it, did you?"

Newly infuriated, Joseph left both dead animals to confront the American. Wading the river did little to cool his suddenly hot blood. "What are you doing here?"

"Saving a poor animal's life." She tossed her head in defiance. Dark ringlets tumbled about her fine features.

"It was injured. It would've died anyway." Joseph gave rein to his anger to hold tight his lust. "You should never leave camp alone."

"You did," she countered from her side of the river.

"I can protect myself." Joseph sheathed his panga and moved the strap so it lay across his back.

"So I noticed." Tia's eyes narrowed with disgust. "How could you kill those soldiers without so much as blinking?"

"How could I not?" Joseph countered, realizing she'd witnessed the battle. "They were laughing. Describing the screams of a young girl as they destroyed her womb." Joseph strode in a large circle. "They had just slaughtered innocent villagers. How could I not kill them?"

Tia raised an eyebrow in query. "Are you trying to convince me or yourself that what you did was right?"

"Do not judge me, woman." Fury shook the finger he pointed at her. "I've already battered myself over and over for the men I've killed these past two years. You have no right to make my pain worse."

The drip of his clothing onto her sandaled feet marked the silence between them. Joseph hadn't meant to confess his personal torture to her, to anyone.

I...oh." Tia registered surprise and lowered her arms. "I didn't realize..."

"There's much you don't realize," he whispered only inches from her beautiful face. Joseph quivered with wanting.

Tia lowered her arms into a less defiant posture. Her wide eyes filled with invitation. Joseph's heart flipped as Tia's lips parted slightly.

All thoughts fled from existence as Joseph succumbed to the desire to taste the pink of her lips, dropping his head to take possession of her mouth. Exotic flavors teased him, tempted him. She tasted of sweet and spice, like innocence and lust.

Tia's moan vibrated against his lips and tongue.

Responding with deep, hungry kisses, anxious hands and full loins, Joseph pulled her tighter into his arms. She felt so good against him. The soft roundness of her breasts against his chest, her bottom in his hands eased his troubled mind, soothed his tortured soul and made his heart pound like the thunder of the falls.

Emotions, thoughts, guilt, pain all whirled away as he sank into oblivion. The Darkness gave way to bright shafts of light that seemed to blaze their way from her body through his.

Tia squeezed his arms beneath hot palms and moaned with urgency.

Joseph's knees weakened. Without breaking their kiss, he lowered her to the ground, anxious to submerge himself completely inside the heat of her. To get that final level of explosive light. Perhaps then he could find complete peace.

Joseph moved on top of Tia. She wriggled beneath him, hips thrusting upward. Her frenzied movements took him dangerously close to release.

Breaking their kiss, Joseph reached between them to lower his zipper.

Tia's moans turned to protests as she shoved him over onto hard earth. "Let's not do this." She moved to a sitting position, panting.

Confused, Joseph lay on his back breathing heavily. "What's wrong?"

Shaking her head, she scrambled to her feet. "It makes everything too complicated. Much too complicated." Tia adjusted her clothing in jerking movements.

Debating whether or not to plead, Joseph stared at the aggravating woman. "You tell me this after you get my blood as hot as an active volcano?"

"I did nothing to encourage your—your—attack," she huffed. "And as for your hot blood, I suggest you cool it with another dunk in the river." Tia finished her adjustments and backed further away.

"You saw me swimming?" Now he was intrigued. She'd been watching him. "How long have you been here?"

"Not long. And, I wasn't watching you. Not exactly." Her chin still angled stubbornly.

Joseph rose slowly to his feet. She'd wanted that kiss as much as he. And she'd wanted more, he could tell. Why was she being so difficult? He gave her a level look and traced a finger down her face. "I wouldn't have minded if you were."

Tia swatted his hand away. "Your hands are stained with blood."

Joseph studied them again, certain he'd cleaned them well, then realized he'd left the cape buffalo to the pack of hyenas that had to be around. "I've got to get that buffalo. A hyena killed it and if I don't gut it, the meat will spoil." He backed away from her, "Can I trust you to go straight back to our camp and request help? I'm sure everyone will consider fresh meat a treat."

She nodded in answer. "That's why you were going to kill it? To feed everyone?"

Enjoying the look of apology in her eyes, Joseph gave a quick nod. A smile turned up the corner of his mouth. God, he liked this woman.

"I'll get help," she said quietly.

Joseph watched until she disappeared into the tall foliage, then went to salvage the buffalo.

By nightfall Tia had purged everything, including the lining, from her stomach. Watching the slaughter of the buffalo had been more than her queasy stomach could take.

It now growled unmercifully at the smell of roasting beef coming from every fire in camp.

Cooked, the meat looked far more appealing and she had no trouble getting down a few bites. "I don't know how you managed this, Sarini." Tia rolled the delicacy around her tongue before swallowing. "But this is the most tender, perfectly seasoned steak I've ever had."

Sarini laughed. "Hunger make it good. I had no spices."

It didn't matter. Tia didn't have to eat rice or pasty oatmeal tonight. She made a glutton of herself without regret.

Spirits were high in the camp that evening. They circled a larger fire tonight, as they shared in the bounty of fresh meat. Soldiers recanted tales of the battle to the Hutu men, a group of women sang to the accompaniment of one of their sons on a small drum. Even Joseph smiled.

He had a beautiful smile, Tia noted. The light of the fire lit the sharp planes of his handsome face. She craved his touch, but didn't dare act on it. She was leaving this country as soon as possible. The last thing she needed was to let herself fall in love with this complicated rebel soldier.

Joseph looked at her in that moment, his eyes searching hers.

She had to admit, it would have been easier to dismiss him if he hadn't confessed his guilt for killing. He'd almost looked vulnerable. Tia turned away as she felt herself warm. She leaned toward Fidele. "How much further is it to Rwanda?" she asked.

"Would you say, two days, Desiré?" Fidele looked past Tia to the man beside her.

Joseph gave an unreadable expression as he answered. "Two days." Then, just so Tia could hear, "You're in a hurry to leave?"

Not when he whispered like that in his deep, sexy voice, leaning so close she could feel his heat more than the fire's. "I came here to help and instead find myself in danger. You were right. I can't make a difference."

"I said that in anger." He struggled for words. "You...you have a great deal to offer."

Tia gave a half laugh. "Yeah? Like what?"

She didn't imagine his eyes roaming her body. Or the way her body reacted. "Never mind," she said. "Don't answer that."

"You've made it easier for us to stay alive, Tia." It was Fidele who spoke. He stared into the fire, a weary expression pulling down his normally cheerful features. "I listen to my wife moan in her sleep, see tears track her cheeks as she pushes herself to take one more step."

Tia looked at Sarini, even now curled in sleep with Denis tucked next to her. The older Zavi children played with the younger ones to keep them from waking their mother.

"She tries because you do," he said quietly. "Because you say tomorrow will be better, because you share as much of the burden for the children as she does." Fidele turned to Tia, his eyes shone with emotion. "Without hope, there is no life."

Tia touched her friend, not knowing what to say. "I...I...don't know..."

"You should stay." It was Joseph's low, rumbling voice this time. "You may prove yourself."

"To whom?" she asked.

"Yourself."

"Joseph, I already know I'm too scared, too tired, too weak to stay." Tia struggled to keep her voice from breaking. "I like having a nice home and hot baths and soft comfortable beds and I want all of it back. And you..." She stopped herself and tried to think of something to say besides how much she wanted him to go with her. "When will the killing be enough for you?" she finally asked.

Joseph shrugged. "I don't know how to do anything else now."

Fidele leaned into the conversation with renewed interest. "Nor do half the men in our countries. Why can't every night be like this one?" He waved his thin, wiry arms at the people gathered around the fire. "Here we have Hutus and Tutsis eating together, laughing together." He stood and addressed the crowd. "Why can't each night be like this?"

Shouts of approval rang out from the crowd. Joseph rose and placed an arm around Fidele's shoulders. "You're a good man, Zavi. With a fine family." He looked fondly on the eight children surrounding their parents. "You're the wealthiest of men."

Suddenly, he looked exhausted. "I must check the perimeters." Strapping his huge blade across his back, he headed for the bush.

It took Tia exactly two seconds to decide to follow.

Joseph turned at the sound of her footsteps. "I told you not to wander from camp," he said with no malice.

"Alone." She crossed her arms with amusement. "You said not to leave camp alone."

His laugh was low and genuine. "So I did." He continued on, pushing aside very large leaves, inviting her to pass beneath his arms.

"Thanks."

They walked companionably for a long while. A slight breeze teased with a hint of the cool night to come. Tia looked past the fingers of leaves to the stars. It occurred to her that the sky was the only thing that looked the same between her country and his.

"Why did you come?" His question interrupted her thoughts.

Tia blew out a long breath. "I don't know," she answered, shaking her head.

Joseph turned on her, halting their walk. "You're not safe with me," he said succinctly.

Tia swallowed the hard lump in her throat. Her pulse began beating like hummingbird wings. "I know."

His hand was on her throat then, caressing, soothing. "I watched you sleep one night," his breath warmed her cheek. "I wondered what it was like to have such peace."

Not capable of answering, Tia closed her eyes and gave in to what she'd wanted all day. His touch. It was wrong to use him like this. She'd be leaving in just a few days and she didn't want to hurt him. But, good Lord, she wanted this. "Joseph, I—"

His mouth covered hers, silencing her words beneath the fervent exploration of his tongue. Her thoughts drowning in a sea of lust.

Moving from her mouth, down her throat to her breasts, he kissed and fondled. He was driving her mad.

And then he stopped, panting, with his forehead against her breasts. "This isn't right. Like you said, it complicates things." He stepped out of her embrace.

"Hell of a time for you to get a conscience, Desiré. What's the matter?"

"If we do this...I won't be able to let you go."

"You have to."

"Why? Because you want all those things you said and I can't give you any of them?"

"Well..."

Joseph rounded on her. His eyes blazed with intense emotion. "Haven't you been here long enough to know that tomorrow may never come? That I can't even guarantee you'll make it to Rwanda?"

Goosebumps rose on her arms. "What do you mean?"

"The Hutu militia guard Rwanda's border. They want no Hutus to return home. Men like your friend, Fidele, are considered traitors."

Dread made Tia's blood run cold. "You're on your way to kill them, aren't you?"

His body was a dark silhouette in the wan light of the quarter moon. "It is why we have come so far," he affirmed.

"Why don't you just stop?"

"Killing?" he asked.

"Yes. And this war," she threw up her arms in frustration. "It wouldn't continue if there weren't any soldiers."

"I am one man. What difference can my quitting make?" There was an edge of irritation in his tone.

"Maybe it would do nothing." Tia proceeded cautiously. "Nothing but give you the peace you claim to want."

"My peace will come soon enough." He was clearly angry now. His fists clenched at his sides. "There's peace in death."

Tia shivered. She understood. He was preparing himself to die. He expected it, wanted it. "You would rather die than be here, wouldn't you?"

She could make out the tense muscles in his jaw.

"What do I have to live for?" This time his voice was quiet as his gaze fell down upon her.

Tia was frightened by the look in his eyes. The one asking her to stay. "I understand you're fighting to avenge your family's deaths." Tia stared at him intently. "You've done that, Joseph. Didn't you say Habyarimana is dead? Go home and find a job. Start a family."

Joseph looked magnificent as moonlight gleamed on his shoulders and the strong lines of his face. "I'd love to."

Suddenly, his arms were about her waist. Tia relaxed in his embrace, placing her head on his shoulder. "I can't stay, Joseph. Please don't ask me to."

"Without you, what will I do?" he whispered.

Squeezing her eyes shut, Tia fought against the desperation in his voice. "Help Fidele. Make sure he makes it home safely."

"He will probably become a beggar," anger sliced his words as he stepped away once again. "That's the way of these things. Who am I to change it?"

Tia understood his anger. He'd offered his heart to her and she'd refused it. "Don't be mad, Joseph. I'm not the right woman for you."

She halted him with an upturned palm when he tried to object. "Just do one favor for me." It was becoming difficult to hold back the hot tears burning her eyes. "Make sure that when Denis Zavi grows up, his choices aren't the same as yours. Kill or be killed."

"Life is a struggle here." A darkness crept into his eyes. "It's best if the child adapts to that fact early on."

"If things continue the way they are, there will never be peace in Africa and the people will always be running." Tia laid a hand on a solid arm. "Don't you feel any empathy for other families who continue to fall victim to this war? Their losses are no different than yours."

Joseph pulled away. "There's nothing I can do about it."

Tia sighed, growing irritated with his increasingly antagonistic mood. "I'm sorry you feel that way, Joseph. I believe a little positive thinking and a good leader can go a long way."

"In America, perhaps." Joseph crossed his arms. "Things are different here. You are right to run back to your home."

"You couldn't be more right." Stomping off, she headed toward camp. At least she hoped she was. She refused to give him the satisfaction of getting lost again.

Six

The ample meal from the previous night had lifted spirits in the camp. They moved with more energy as they headed down the last leg of the mountain toward the Rwandan border.

Sarini's leftover meat lay wrapped and stowed in baskets. What couldn't be preserved remained for the scavengers.

The day appeared harshly bright to Tia. She hoped they'd make the border soon. She'd had enough of this country.

She had taken pains not to look in Joseph's direction all morning. Perhaps, he was right. This country couldn't be held to the same standard as her own. In Zaire, death was the only season and peace happened only in fairy tales.

By late afternoon, the trail had turned to a steep downgrade. Tia's knees threatened to give out several times as she slipped and slid down the steep mountain.

Joseph positioned himself directly behind her. Tia knew it was his not-so-subtle way of watching her. Loathing his attention was simply adolescent, but she had no intention of falling down another mountain. She placed each step carefully, evading every root and vine in her path. It seemed ages before they finally reached bottom.

As they finished their descent, a mob of angry Rwandans became visible several hundred yards down a pitted road. Tia recognized the peeled, white building they swarmed as a store house for Feed the World. Tarps held off the ground by sticks formed makeshift tents and the odd blanket and baskets littering the ground proclaimed this location another refugee camp.

Fidele stood beside her, placing Denis on the ground to stand on his own. "Must be low on rations," came his explanation of the scene.

Tia could feel the desperation of the people. No gunshots or mortars pounded the skies, but starvation was just as great a threat to their survival.

Joseph brushed past Tia toward the melee, flanked by a few of his men.

Bolongo hung back. "Bloody Hutu animals," he sneered, not bothering to hide his disdain.

"You'd be a little desperate if you were starving." Tia said defensively.

"I'd sooner die than turn beggar." He spat at Fidele's feet, looked in distaste at the Hutus around him, then loped off, reluctantly, to join his commander.

Fidele studied the spittle that lay within a fraction of his dusty sandal. Without a word, he turned, grabbed Denis's hand and walked back toward his family.

Tia tagged after him openmouthed. "Why didn't you say something? You just let him talk about your people without even a rebuttal."

Fidele turned and gave her a curious grin. "For a woman who hates war, you certainly like to pick fights," he countered.

"I do not." Tia rounded on him. "But there's such a thing as standing up for yourself. Showing some pride in your heritage."

"Pride is built upon the strength of a man's actions, not the fight of his words." Fidele spoke with a quiet wisdom. "Had the men in power remembered that, we wouldn't be here today witnessing our people's desperation for their next meal." He inclined his sweat-beaded head toward the chaos of the refugee camp.

Tia turned back to the grim scene. Of course, he was right. Verbal sparring with Bolongo would serve no useful purpose. She sighed. "You're right, Fidele. I just wish he didn't make me so—"

Suddenly, Bolongo leapt onto a long serving table in the midst of the throng. The aid workers fell back against the storage shed, helpless as the ugly man began to yell and beat back starving Hutus with the butt of his rifle. A gleeful, sinister expression twisted his face.

Tia's blood raced as she pushed her way toward the table.

The rifle butt connected with the temple of a young boy, making a sickening cracking sound as Tia climbed up next to Bolongo. Grabbing at the rifle, she tried to wrangle it from his hands.

"Crazy woman." Bolongo pulled the weapon free of her hands. "Stay out of my way!" He raised the gun to strike her, clearly meaning to crush her skull.

Tia covered her head, felt the table shake under the thud of new weight, and toppled onto the tabletop.

"What are you doing?" The thunder of Joseph's anger stopped the stampeding Rwandan refugees and everyone else in their tracks. "These people need your help, not more pain," he yelled at his second-in-command.

Tia could see the activity through Joseph's long legs as he ripped Bolongo's rifle free and shoved him to the ground. Tia wanted to applaud as the breath exploded violently from Bolongo's lungs and dust rose. She slid her way from between her rescuer's legs and dropped to the ground, happy to watch Leonard gasp for air.

Leonard labored to his feet. Before Tia knew it, he'd grabbed her wrists and brought them up from her sides. "Why're your fists balled up?" His English was spoken with cockney accent rather than Joseph's sing-songy lilt. Perhaps, he'd grown up around someone from Great Britain. "Thinking of takin' a swipe at me, too?" The fall hadn't adjusted his nasty attitude a bit.

Tia pulled her wrists through his thumbs and forefingers in the one self-defense move she remembered from a class she took long ago. "No. I'm not going to hit you." She folded her arms to prevent an accidental punch. "And

I would appreciate it if you kept your hands off me." Just beyond Bolongo's right shoulder, she could see Fidele's watchful gaze.

Joseph dropped to the ground and tension between the three of them electrified the air. "Don't touch her or the rest of these people again, Leonard," he warned.

Blood-specked spittle ran from the man's ugly lips. "Why do you defend these bloody animals? They killed your family and mine. Burned them without a second thought. They deserve no mercy." His eyes were as red as his blood.

"You've no right to question me." Joseph's eyes turned to vicious slits. "I remember the men who killed our families. All of them were older than that boy."

The young man Bolongo had struck lay motionless on the ground. Tia sank to her knees and felt his throat for a pulse.

There was none.

Grief seized her for the child she didn't know. She sat back on her heels and covered her face. Tears stung the backs of her eyes.

"Why're you crying?" It was Bolongo's voice. "You should all be happy now." He yelled at the crowd of Hutus. "One less mouth to feed. More for you, you filthy boars!"

Tia wiped her face and stood to face the man she'd come to hate. Though his glare was laced with venom, she met him levelly. "I'm sorry your family was killed if it's made you into this monster. But, you've no right to sit in judgment of these people. No right to kill innocent children."

"You think Desiré here is such a prince?" He gestured toward his fuming commander. "He was a killing machine when I met him. That's what I liked about him. Why I followed him. But since you came, he's become weak and soft. What magic are you weaving over him, American witch?"

"Enough!" Joseph pulled Leonard by his collar and whispered something to the man between clenched teeth.

Though she stood close by, Tia couldn't hear Joseph's words. Their effect on Leonard, however, was immediate. He held his tongue, straightened his uniform and walked off a ways to sulk beneath a tree.

Joseph gave Tia a searching look. "You all right?" His question more a command, he sought her answer with concerned eyes.

She nodded. "How do you put up with him?"

He offered no answer, just touched her cheek so briefly she wondered if she'd imagined it.

And then, he was gone.

Striding through the crowd of refugees, Joseph barked orders to his men. Once again, he was about the business of creating order from chaos.

Children moved in wide-eyed obedience as his men guided them to the front of the food line. Women and men fell in place behind the little ones, yielding to the authority in Joseph's thunderous voice.

Once the people were in place, he organized the aid workers. In no time, they had huge cookpots full of mushy grain ready to ladle.

Tia stood transfixed as Joseph turned his wide, straight shoulders in her direction. "You should help serve," he stated matter-of-factly. "That's why you're here, isn't it?" A hint of humor softened the sarcasm of his query.

Without a word, Tia walked over and playfully lifted the ladle from his finger. She was near enough to see the beads of sweat that glistened on his ebony cheek and jaws. Within hearing of his steady breathing. Close enough to reach inside his opened shirt collar and feel the plated muscles of his chest.

She didn't touch him, though. Instead, she gave him a look intended to make him think she would.

His eyes darkened with lust. It was a dangerous game. One she wouldn't be able to stop if it began.

"Careful," he leaned closer. "If I get my hands on you again, I won't be able to stop."

He'd had the same killer look when he'd kissed her on the riverbank. Finding it just as compelling to be held by his dark, dangerous stare as his taut, muscular arms, Tia basked in his attention a while longer. "Maybe I wouldn't want you to." She wished he'd kiss her again, but knew it couldn't happen.

A small cough alerted her to the child before her.

Joseph turned away.

Tia went about the business of being an aid worker. She ladled sticky goo into a bowl while the little girl studied every move. Dark, dusty skin clung pitifully to small ribs and stretched to fit an extended abdomen. A dirty wrap-around skirt hugged slight hips and dropped to the girl's knobby knees. A poster child for malnutrition, Tia thought sadly.

Managing a smile, Tia offered the meager meal.

The girl beamed an absolutely gorgeous smile and moved aside to partake of her feast.

With a portion of beef still digesting inside her, Tia felt wrought with guilt as she continued to sling paste on one plate after another. Too bad they couldn't have brought more of the meat with them.

Apparently the same thought had occurred to Joseph, who had his men passing out leftovers to those at the back of the line. Touched beyond words, Tia regretted even more that she had to leave soon.

It took over an hour to feed the starving refugees. Portions had gotten progressively smaller toward the end, making Joseph's generous donation of cape buffalo an even more meaningful gesture.

When everyone was fed, Tia sank against the wall of the depot, exhausted. Joseph had disappeared some time ago. Hopefully to get rid of Bolongo who was also absent.

"Well, it's been a pleasure to work with you." Her partner for the past sixty minutes, a tall, frizzy blond man with kind hazel eyes offered his hand to her. "Jean-Claude," he said by way of introduction, his accent richly French.

"Cristiana. Call me Tia."

Jean-Claude slid his backside down the wall of the aid station, mimicking Tia's position. "So, Tia. How is it you're still in Africa? Relief workers were to be evacuated earlier this week."

"I missed my boat." Tia smiled.

"Literally?" he queried.

She nodded. "Fell into Lake Tanganyika."

"Really?" His eyes lit with humor. "How perfectly comical."

"Maybe now," Tia had to admit. "But not at the time."

"To be sure." Jean-Claude sobered. "Nicole and I simply refused to leave."

Tia's eyes traveled to the calm, competent woman who nursed the scrapes and gashes of those wounded in the stampede. "At least there's no warring here."

"Not for the moment. It worries me to see these Tutsis, though."

"Why?"

"About a mile outside this refugee camp is a group of Hutu militia." His hazel eyes narrowed with worry as he looked down a dirt road, as if he could see them. "They're keeping us here. Pent up like swine."

Uneasiness crept up Tia's spine. "They won't let us through to Kigali?" Joseph was right. "My friends live there and I'm trying to get back to America."

Jean-Claude gave her a level gaze. "So far, they've killed every Hutu and Tutsi who's crossed them."

"Tutsis, I understand." Though she suddenly feared for Joseph. "But, why won't they let their own people inside Rwanda?" she asked, though she knew the answer.

"They think it's treasonous to return to their homes as long as a Tutsi rules," Jean-Claude confirmed.

Tia buried her face in her hands. Exhaustion pressed like a weight upon her shoulders. "The stupidity of this war never ceases to amaze me." She faced her companion. "I don't suppose I stand a chance of getting out of this hellhole simply because I'm American?"

He shook his head. "It's doubtful. You'll be considered guilty by association, as my wife and I are. And worse, all of us will starve if the militia continue to hold back our supplies."

"Wonderful," she sighed. "We sit here and starve or push forward and risk being killed." She shook her head. "What lovely alternatives."

"Ah, but there's another." Jean-Claude held up a finger in mock humor. "It seems a virus is going around as well." His eyes lost a little of their vibrancy. "Nicole has saved some. Lost many more."

Tia sat a moment longer to build enough energy to make it to her feet. She'd come to Africa to be of service—to help in some way. So far, she'd done nothing. Less than nothing. It would be impossible to return to America with the fate of these people on her conscience. "Something has to be done," she spoke her resolution aloud.

"We're doing all we can."

"It's not enough." She scanned the sea of starving, sick people who'd eaten barely enough to sustain their lives today.

Jean-Claude stood at her side. "What can you do?"

"I'll get to Kigali, contact my mother. She's a United States Senator who can move some high-powered butts in Washington to get help here."

Jean-Claude narrowed his eyes. "Careful you don't go spreading that news around."

Tia frowned. "Why not? These people need hope—something positive to cling to."

"You have a parent in a prominent position. Many around here are desperate enough to use you to extort money from your family."

Tia surveyed the weak, thin Hutus. "These people aren't hostile. None of them would think to take me hostage."

Jean-Claude nodded. "Maybe not these, but what of the ugly man. The one you fought with?"

She looked for Bolongo under the tree he'd taken refuge under earlier. He wasn't there. In fact, he was nowhere to be seen. "He knows about my mother." In fact, everyone knew because of the stories she'd told the children.

She shrugged it off. "If he was going to extort money from me or my family, he would've done it by now," she reasoned.

Jean-Claude tilted his fuzzy blond head. "Perhaps. Stay close to your Tutsi commander just the same."

"My Tutsi commander?"

Her companion's eyes twinkled once more. "I could be mistaken—usually I'm not——but I sense a chemistry between you two. True?"

Like an Einstein formula, she wanted to confess. It seemed best not to admit it, though. After all, nothing would come of it. The arrival of Jean-Claude's wife provided enough distraction to get Tia off the hook.

"Ah, darling," the man wrapped the slight woman in a long arm and drew her in. "I'd like you to meet Tia. She's been working in Uvira and is now trying to get home to America."

Nicole swept back an errant strand of brunette hair and offered her hand. "It's a pleasure," she said in a sweet, soft voice laced with exhaustion. "I wish you luck." Her grip was surprisingly strong for its bird-like structure.

"Likewise," Tia smiled. "I hate to meet and run, but I've got some business to attend."

Nicole nodded and leaned against her husband.

"Take care of yourself," Jean-Claude called after her.

Tia waved and thought what a nice couple they made.

With renewed purpose, she made her way to where Joseph and his men had set up their camp.

Joseph sat against an old stump, studying a map spread to his side. He had to hear her approach, but he didn't look up.

She planted her feet and put her hands on her hips. Taking a deep breath, she swallowed her pride. "I need your help."

Joseph leaned back to assess her. A slow smile stretched across his face. When wearing a scowl this man was handsome, but a full-fledged smile enhanced the strong lines of his face to devastating levels. "You're asking for my help before you jump into trouble? How unusual."

It was Tia's turn to smile. "So, you are capable of humor. Who would've thought?" She sank to the ground to talk with him. "I'm on a mission."

"Another?" Joseph's eyes were dark with promise as an orange and black sunset seared the sky behind him. Intimacy settled with the falling night. "Who do you want to save now?"

She wanted desperately to save herself from falling further in love with the warrior——unfortunately, it was much too late. "The Hutus, of course." She fanned herself with her hand to keep down the unexpected flush creeping up her neck.

Joseph cocked his head and uttered a low moan. "Are you warm?"

Boiling.

Tia nodded as she eyed the wide expanse of chest exposed beneath Joseph's uniform. It stretched against its remaining buttons. It took her a moment to get herself together. "You were right about the Hutu militia. One of the aid workers says they're a mile outside of camp," she finally managed.

"I know."

"I need to get past them."

The smile disappeared from his face. His expression turned grim. "You know we are here to fight. It would be too dangerous to take you along."

"I have to get to Kigali. These people are going to die—"

"Continue dying," he corrected. "Several hundred are buried just past the brush there."

Tia followed his pointing finger and fought down panic. "All the more reason to get help fast," she insisted.

"Wait until I take care of the Hutus, then I'll come back for you."

Tia sighed. "How long will that take?"

"I don't know. A day."

"Not to hurt your pride or anything, but what if you don't win?"

Joseph smiled. "I always win."

Tia relaxed a little. "You do, don't you?"

He took her chin in a strong hand and looked straight into her eyes.

She couldn't breathe. Couldn't move.

"I promise to get you to Kigali. And to get you home to America." He paused, searching for something. "If you're sure that's what you want."

"Lately I'm not sure what I want," she answered honestly.

His smile reappeared.

"You were right when you said I haven't made much of a difference in this country. Well, I have a mother who can. Before I leave, I want to give these people more than food and water. I want to give them back their homes."

"I've never met anyone so full of good intentions." His kiss was gentle as he brushed her lips with his own.

"I've gotta go." Because she wanted to stay, Tia rose and headed back to the Zavi family.

Joseph watched her walk away. She didn't belong here. He'd thought it before, but knew it now. It was too harsh a life to live in Rwanda and Zaire.

A woman of such beauty deserved hot baths, combs, perfumes and mansions. If only such things were at his disposal, Joseph would lay them at her feet. Feet clad in fine gold sandals, not old tires and jungle vines. If she stayed, maybe one day..."

If she stayed, she would die.

Starting tonight, Joseph would get no rest watching out for Leonard Bolongo's return. He knew his second well enough to know he wouldn't suffer today's humiliation without retaliation. Unfortunately, it could be Tia he targeted.

Leaving his tent, Joseph moved toward a tall group of bushes. It would be harder for Bolongo to sneak up on him here. Tia's sleeping blanket was within sight and only a few paces away. Joseph settled with his back to a sturdy trunk and waited.

Hushed voices conversed in small clusters about camp. A small child complained of hunger while its mother tried to still his cries with singing. In the midst of the voices, he heard Tia telling a story to the Zavi children. Many others came round to hear as she punctuated her words with big gestures and an animated tone.

Joseph listened and wondered at the beautiful American. She was a storyteller, a griot. One capable of touching hearts with her words—of making children laugh in the midst of horror. One capable of stirring the dark heart of a warrior with the sweet innocence of her convictions.

When he'd taken up the cause of the rebels, Joseph's only thought had been to shift power to the Tutsis. Now he knew that once that happened, one war would end and another would begin. Someone needed to bridge the disparity between those who have and those who have nothing and treat all people equally no matter what tribe they belong to.

This dream was worth fighting for. He knew it yesterday when Tia had said it. Hell, he'd known it for a very long time, but had refused to act on it.

Killing Hutu militiamen and Zairian soldiers had done nothing to assuage the emptiness inside him. Perhaps building a new government would.

Tia was right. He had to have something to live for. And new possibilities flooded his mind. He'd had two years of college before the war, certainly his schooling would be seen as an asset to the rebel leadership. He could help build a new nation. One equitable to every tribe.

A dark shadow approached Joseph's tent, damping his thoughts. Instinctively, he put a hand to his gun.

"Commander?" The hateful tone identified Bolongo.

From his shielded vantage point, Joseph sat watching his second clench and unclench his fists. Odd. Where were his weapons? In the past year and a half, Bolongo always had a knife or gun strapped to himself. Not now.

One of the young recruits walked up to Bolongo. "I think the Commander's securing the perimeter, Leonard. What's going on?" Their voices drifted clearly across the camp.

"I radioed the base this afternoon. They said Jeeps would be waiting for us in Cyungugu. We can ride the remainder of the way to Kigali."

"Good. My boots are about worn through. They won't last another day. "I'll wait up for the Commander if you don't want to face him."

"What does that mean?" Bolongo demanded. "You think I'm afraid of him?"

"Well, no...I just thought."

"Don't think!" Bolongo pushed a finger into the man's chest and loped off toward his own tent.

Wariness crept up Joseph's neck like a cold wind. It was obvious Leonard was straining to hold his peace. Which wasn't normal. Something was up and Joseph could feel it.

Darkness fell over the camp, and with it, an eerie chill. A restlessness pervaded the unusually quiet plain on the border of Rwanda and Zaire. No monkeys screeched in trees, no owls hooted their songs to the moon. The sounds of war had diminished.

Joseph stretched his arms and arched his back several times to stay alert. At odd times in the thick of the night, refugees and soldiers alike, added wood to their fires. Twice, Bolongo's shadowy lope had wandered the camp. Never toward Tia, though he'd drifted close to Joseph's tent a time or two. On both occasions, he'd skulked away as if thinking better of approaching.

Near daybreak, Joseph's eyes felt like sandpaper and his bones held the chill of the damp night. His uneasiness refused to disappear, even with the new morning. Looking through the dusk and mist toward Tia for the thousandth time, Joseph stretched the kinks from his back. If Leonard hadn't tried anything by now, she was surely safe.

Tia shifted under her blanket. Stopped. Shifted a few times more before finally shaking off the green cloth and heading toward the brush.

Grinning, Joseph decided she'd be safe enough. He hoped she had the gun he'd given her in a handy place. Stiffly, but silently, he crossed the turf to slide inside his tent, and make it appear he'd been there all night.

Within fifteen minutes, footsteps approached his dome. "Commander?"

"Yes." Joseph pushed his way out to see his young recruit. "What is it, David?"

"The men are preparing to leave for Cyungugu. Bolongo said trucks will be waiting for us there."

"Fine. Check our ammunition. We may be in for quite a fight."

"Yes, sir." The boy turned with more ceremony than was necessary and began organizing the troops.

Joseph nearly chuckled. The boy was trying out for the Second-In-Command position. Apparently, he didn't think Leonard would be around much longer.

Joseph found the thought appealing.

At that moment, his current second came bounding over. "I'll take a group ahead and see how many Hutu dogs—"

Joseph's glare halted him for a moment.

"—militia we'll have to contend with."

Pushing to his feet, Joseph regarded the man. "You're in a good mood considering yesterday's scuffle."

Leonard bounced nervously from foot to foot. "I lost my head, Commander. It's all over now."

He was lying. Joseph didn't like the way the man's eyes shifted from the brush to the ground to the camp. "What are you up to, Leonard? What game are you playing?"

"Nothing," he countered belligerently. "I just want to reach headquarters and get some rest. Why do I have to be up to something?" Leonard spat for emphasis.

Joseph wondered if he should kill him now rather than worry about him. "Prepare to leave. Make sure we have enough rations for two days."

"And how will we get past the Hutu militia?" His tone turned sweetly sarcastic. "Will we be sneaking up on tip-toes again?"

"Actually, no." Joseph tilted his head in thought. "I'm going to try an experiment."

Complete befuddlement altered Bolongo's ugly features. "What kind of experiment?"

"Negotiation."

"That's ridiculous." Bolongo ground his teeth until they nearly sparked. "It won't work." Pivoting angrily, he stormed back to his tent.

Joseph thought on his last word. It would certainly take more courage to talk their way past the Hutus rather than kill them. Could it be done? He was feeling bold. Daring. No harm in trying.

Tia zipped up her shorts and tried to keep them up about her waist by pulling her belt in tighter. She'd lost weight. It was about the best thing she could say about her romp around Africa, she yawned and rubbed sleep-drugged eyes. A few steps toward camp was all she took before men appeared from the shadows to take hold of her arms and legs and lifted her off the ground. A nasty tasting rag filled her mouth as she opened it to scream. She nearly gagged as they ran with her deeper into the bush.

What was happening? And where was Joseph?

Twisting and turning in her captors' arms, Tia struggled to break free. No good. Where was Joseph? He'd always been there to save her before. Where was he now?

Seven

Joseph surveyed his assembled men. Tents were packed, as were their rations. Each man stood ready with his backpack awaiting orders as gray smoke from dormant fires spiraled against the lightening sky.

Something was wrong. All men were accounted for, including Leonard. But something didn't feel right deep inside Joseph's gut. "Let's go men. And, remember, only fire when I signal. We'll kill as a last resort this mission."

Leonard grunted his disapproval, but led the group into the bush. Joseph gave one last look toward Fidele's family. Many were moving around. He didn't see Tia, but the mist made it difficult to distinguish individuals at this distance.

Fidele pushed back the tarp, awakening to find his wife leaning against a tall tree. He noticed the bare camp where Desiré and his men had slept. "Have the Tutsis moved out so early?"

Sarini squinted against the mist. "Yes. Tia say Joseph Desiré will clear out militia today. I hope they successful."

Noting her weary expression, Fidele moved to sit beside her. Placing an arm around her shoulders, he pulled her close, concerned that he could feel bones through her clothing. "I know you're tired, my love. Hold on. We'll be home soon."

A faint reply was all she could manage.

Fidele kissed her forehead. She was sweating, though the morning was cool. "Are you ill, Sarini?" he asked alarmed.

This time, there was no reply.

Denis came to sit by his mother. "Where Tia? She give medicine to help."

Her blanket lay in a pile, but Tia was nowhere to be found. "Maybe she went into the bush to relieve herself," Fidele surmised. "Go get the white woman who gives medicine," he urged Denis.

The boy was off and running toward the aid station as fast as his little legs would move. Fidele called his older girls to him. "Get water from the river. Boil some to make it clean. We must take care of your mother." The girls took off as Fidele laid his wife on their piled blankets. Cold fear gripped his heart. Losing Sarini would mean losing his world. He must pray to the gods for their mercy.

❖❖❖

Joseph's trek into Rwanda was heralded by the crimson-streaked clouds of dawn. At once, a stunning tribute to God's fathomless creativity and a grim but accurate reflection of spilled African blood. Perhaps, no more had to be shed. At least, not today.

Joseph marched purposefully toward Cyungugu, a plan playing in his mind. He looked back to find Bolongo conversing with two of his more senior soldiers. Both men looked deeply agitated.

Growing more and more uneasy, Joseph dropped back to see if he could hear what they spoke about. As suspected, the conversation ended as he drew closer. "You men should stay alert. Keep quiet."

"Aye, Commander," the two soldiers said in unison. Bolongo simply nodded his odd-shaped head. His eyes gleamed as if holding back a treasured secret.

"Go on ahead." Joseph waved Bolongo past to separate him from the others. Being the first to encounter the enemy would make him less comfortable, he decided.

"Commander?"

"Yes, David?"

"Is something going on?" the young man asked.

"More than we know, I fear," he said quietly. "Stay alert."

"Aye."

Not far down the road, Bolongo stopped. "We've been spotted," he said to the men's questioning looks.

The bush shook noisily. A red sash, identifying the man as a Hutu scout, disappeared into the dense shrubbery.

"He's gone to alert his troop," David said.

"Remain calm," Joseph instructed, taking the lead from Bolongo. "Don't shoot until I say."

Moving forward, they could hear shouting. Then heavy footsteps of running men. Joseph's heart raced, but he struggled not to pull his gun from his belt.

It took only a matter of minutes for Hutu guards to race upon them, rifles ready. One man was short and broad, the other tall and lean with missing front teeth.

Joseph mentally checked the location of his gun, comforted by the weight of his panga strapped across his back, he planted an easy grin on his face. "Good day," he heralded the guards.

"Don't come any closer, Tutsi dog," the shorter man scowled.

"Let's kill them now, Commander." Leonard spoke from the side of his wide mouth. "Before they know what hits them."

"You." The taller man pointed his weapon at Leonard. "Step aside."

Joseph laid a firm hand on Bolongo's shoulder. "He's not going anywhere. We don't want trouble. Only to discuss safe passage of some of your people."

The two guards gave each other a quick glance. "It's true? You hold Hutu civilians captive?" he spoke in French.

Imminent danger crackled up Joseph's back and neck like a lightning bolt. "I hold no one captive."

"Lying Tutsi!" The tall guard spat through the gap in his teeth with the violence of his words. "Release your man. Now."

"What the hell's going on, Leonard?" Joseph asked as Leonard went to stand with the Hutus. The two men who'd huddled with him earlier also went to the other side.

Mutinous hyena dung. Joseph would have to kill today after all.

"I hear the American woman's family will pay lots of money to have their daughter back." Leonard gave a gap-toothed smile that spread like venom across his face. "I offered her to the Hutus."

"You heard wrong." Joseph had to think fast. "She's no daughter of a United States dignitary. She makes that stuff up for the kids," Joseph insisted. "You'll get paid when we take over Zaire. Kabila has promised us all top positions in his cabinet."

"Why wait?" Leonard laughed. "Besides, I have proof." He pulled a sloppily-folded flyer from his pocket and opened it up for all to see.

Horrified, Joseph took in the lovely picture of Tia and the text requesting any information for the whereabouts of the U.S. Senator's daughter who disappeared in Zaire a week ago. They were willing to pay $10,000 in U.S. currency for anyone with information.

"My parents are here?" Tia appeared from behind bush, hands behind her back, a huge monster of a man holding tight to her arm.

"Not here. Kigali." Leonard grinned wickedly.

"I'll happily go with you," Tia said. "You don't have to tie me up."

Bolongo seared her with his look. "If you walk in like you'd been on a lark, d'ya think they'd give me any money?"

"They would if I told them to."

"Sure you would." Bolongo took her chin in his hand. "Just 'cause we're such good buddies, eh?"

Tia turned her head from the man's filthy hands. "Just so I can go home," she said with controlled anger.

Joseph registered the placement of every visible Hutu as he tried to calculate his next move.

The large Hutu, clearly the commander, pulled Tia away from Leonard. "Let's get with it," he said in halting French. "You travel to Kigali. Tell American parents you know where their daughter is kept. We will meet you in village outside of city. We give woman for money." He jerked Tia's arms which looked like a doll's in the large man's grip and dragged her back from the path.

Tia gave a pleading look toward Joseph.

He gave her a slight nod, hoping to ease her fear. It was clear they wouldn't harm her. At least not until they got the reward money.

"What about the Tutsis?" the short guard asked his ranking officer.

"Kill them. Not kill them. Don't matter." The large man waved dismissively as he headed toward a large tent.

"Kill that one if you don't want any more trouble." Leonard pointed at Joseph with a smile. "Kill him and you'll free the Hutus he holds hostage."

Joseph saw a determined look pass between the guards.

Smiling, Leonard gave a mock salute to Joseph. "So long, Commander." He left for the Hutu camp as well.

A quiet uncertainty mixed with anger as Joseph tried to find a way out. If he fired now, they'd be laid flat by the dozen Hutus they could see, and the unknown number they couldn't.

Perspiration seeped from every pore on Joseph's body. Not so much by the heat of the progressing day, but by the risky situation he'd gotten himself into. Get past the Hutus without bloodshed, hah. His fingers itched to get at his panga. "Let us pass. We're only headed to collect our vehicles and then we'll be gone. We hold no Hutus hostage. If you don't believe me, go back a mile and see for yourselves."

"It's a trick," the short man said, sighting his rifle on Joseph.

Joseph began to laugh. His men and the guards all looked at him in disbelief. When he was certain he had their attention, he doubled over, holding onto his stomach, as if he couldn't control his mirth.

Falling to the ground, Joseph rolled with another fit of laughter to shield his actions. He pulled his gun from his side as he rolled onto his belly, then pointed and shot as he rolled onto his back.

The two guards dropped like overripe fruit, their faces still frozen with surprise.

"See if you can find our jeeps and reinforcements," he instructed his men. "We have to reach Kigali before Bolongo."

"That was genius, Commander," David said as he trotted alongside Joseph into the bush.

"Later, man. We've got work to do." Joseph headed toward their rendezvous point, hoping Bolongo and the Hutu commander thought him dead. Once they found the guards, things would get very complicated.

Joseph and his remaining men found the vehicles parked haphazardly around a small clearing. Adebo and his men were nowhere to be found. Maybe his fellow rebels were dead by the Hutu's hand.

"I see you're eyeing my jeeps." Everyone turned at the stranger's voice. A well-dressed man, decidedly American, exited a nearby tent.

"These autos belong to us." Joseph stepped up to the man.

"Wrong. They were sold to me by some men dressed similarly to you." The man eyed Joseph's uniform. "Except a bit less worn, I'd say."

Would today hold nothing but mutiny and treachery, Joseph thought in irritation.

The man pulled out a long, thin cigarette, tapped it against his gold case, lit it, and blew a long stream of smoke in Joseph's direction. "They said a man named Desiré would be along claiming they were his."

"They were right. Here I am." Joseph planted his feet further apart. "And I'll be damned if I buy back my own merchandise."

"Apparently, you've been in the jungle too long, Desiré. You see, this is what's called a business transaction," he over-enunciated each vowel.

Joseph wanted to smash his smug face.

"Once money is exchanged, so is ownership," the man continued. "Now, if you'd like to make me a deal, we can discuss this further."

Joseph reached back, grabbed the handle of his panga and brought the broad blade forward. "I'll let you live while I take the autos. How's that for a deal?"

Unmoved, the man let out a shrill whistle. Within moments, a small band of gun-wielding men entered the clearing. It was Joseph's dozen soldiers to about thirty bedraggled men whose allegiance was clearly the money the man had to throw at them.

"You may have greater numbers, sir. But we're skilled in killing. Your men are merely beggars with guns." Joseph tilted his blade so that the light glinted on it.

For the first time, the man didn't seem as sure of himself. "You've got a point." Flicking his cigarette, he gestured for his men to stand down. Approaching Joseph, he offered a hand. "The name's Algood. Mason Algood. I know when I've been bested."

Joseph was too stunned to shake. "You're related to Tia?"

Mason cocked his head. "Tia? She's my wife. How do you know her? Is she here? Her parents are desperate to know if she's safe."

"Your wife?"

"So to speak." Mason gestured ambiguously. "Do you know where she is?"

"Yes." Joseph glared at the man. Tia had said nothing of a husband. "If I don't find her soon, she may die."

"Then, take a jeep. As many as you like." Mason raced to jump inside one himself.

Joseph threw his panga in the back of an auto, barely waiting for three of his men to join him before taking off. A husband. What kind of a man would let his wife go off to Africa, in the middle of a war, all by herself? A worthless one. He didn't deserve her, the polished weasel.

Leonard trudged angrily between his Hutu escorts. How could he have known Desiré would escape? The Hutus should blame their own weak men, not him.

Now they didn't trust him to bring back the money from Kigali. Not that he ever intended to. Damn Joseph just the same. He always had a way of messing things up. But not for long. He would get rid of him just as soon as he found the American's parents.

He and his escorts had left the bush behind a few miles back. They passed through a village where mud houses with cone-shaped thatch roofs dotted the landscape. The people were singing and talking around a large fire. Children played or slept near their mothers. Suddenly heartsick for the family he'd lost, Leonard let his pain turn to bitterness. Hutu dogs. They would pay, too. They would pay.

He pressed back the sour taste of hate all the way through the village and into the city of Kigali.

The Hutus had moved their camp in the short span of time they'd been gone.

It was a smart move, Joseph thought. They must know he lived and probably thought he'd bring more Tutsis to the fight.

"What now, Commander?" It was David asking as he pushed aside sweat. The day had turned viciously hot and humid.

"We've got to find them," Joseph replied, taking a swig of water from his canteen. "They can't have gone far. There wasn't time."

"What about our reinforcements?"

"Gone. Probably in Kigali getting drunk with the money they got from our jeeps." Joseph held the boy's shoulder as he spoke. "We're on our own. Let's move."

It was hot inside the big tent. And the cloth in her mouth tasted foul. Tia, who'd been sitting for hours, shifted on the hard ground in a vain attempt to get the feeling back in her rear.

The only other person present was a fidgety Leonard Bolongo who'd just been escorted inside a few minutes ago. He tossed down the last of his beer, crushed the can, then pushed to his feet. First he looked outside the tent, then glared at Tia.

As best as she could with a gag, she returned a hate-filled stare. Leonard wasn't being held prisoner, but she could tell he wanted out of the Hutu camp as badly as she.

A large shadow fell inside the tent. It was the big Hutu commander. Leonard turned to face him. "Well?"

"It all there. You a lucky man." The man's wide nose flared along with his smile. "Glad I did not kill you."

"Great. You can barter with that American for weapons now. I'll be on my way."

"The woman?" The large Hutu drilled Tia with his lusty gaze.

"Keep her. What the hell do I care?" Bolongo said. "I got my share of the money and her parents have troops looking for you at your old camp site. My business is done."

As much as she didn't want to go with Leonard, Tia really didn't want to stay. She protested behind her gag.

The Hutu stepped aside to let Bolongo go, then turned his attention in Tia's direction.

His look was leering and giddy. "If he no want you. I find good use." He laughed.

Tia pushed further back against the tent, cringing. She had a sneaking suspicion whatever he had in mind didn't involve money.

The Hutu advanced on her. Lifting her up by an elbow, he escorted her roughly across the compound and inside another, larger tent.

Empty beer cans were scattered about, the fold-a-way bed was unmade and a table was stacked with papers and dog-eared maps. To Tia's disappointment, she was directed toward the bed.

"Sit," he ordered.

She sat on the edge trying to decide how to reason with him. If she convinced him she posed no threat—and no profit to him—he might let her go.

A small generator whirred softly as the Hutu pulled a beer from a midget refrigerator near the fold out table. He plopped down into a chair and sucked down a huge mouthful of liquid, all the while eyeing her as if she was Playmate of the Month.

Skin crawling, Tia averted her eyes. She noted the white, crusty stains on the green wool blanket. Semen. Queasiness took a leap inside her stomach.

Forcing herself to remain calm, Tia knew she'd suffocate in her own vomit if she allowed herself to get sick. If only he'd remove the gag.

A resounding belch filled the tent as the big man flattened the now empty can between his palms. He rose to his feet and approached the bed.

Tia's pulse quickened and a dull ache began in her throat.

"You pretty," he said with lust burning in his eyes. His touch was rough and left a faint odor of his beverage on her cheek.

Tia tried to turn away, but he persisted. His hand traveled down her throat and came to rest on her left breast.

Her screams of protest were muted against the taut cloth in her mouth. Panic rose with full force when he closed his eyes, threw his head back and kneaded the soft flesh through her clothing.

Tia pushed her way to her feet and ran.

He caught her by the rope binding her wrists and pulled her against him. "No be scared," he said in a hoarse whisper. "Won't hurt."

Again, he closed his eyes. Lost in need, he began to grope her in earnest. Now his touch bruised as it grabbed tender flesh. His patience with her clothing wore thin and he forced a hand beneath her tank top and attempted to find the clasp of her bra.

Tia continued to struggle, to shake her head, to plead without words that he stop. Not only did he continue, but he seemed oblivious to her attempts to pull free of his unwanted touch.

At that moment, one of the Hutu's soldiers pushed through the opening in the tent. Making no secret of his pleasure in seeing Tia being mauled, he spoke quickly in his native language.

Whatever his question, the large Hutu answered with a nod and a grunt, then shooed him away with his massive hand.

Before the man could turn and leave, he was grabbed from behind and his throat slit cleanly from one side to the other.

Leonard stepped forward to grab a bag lying on the floor. "Sorry to interrupt. But, I decided to take a larger share." He ran out as the Hutu thundered across the tent.

Finally, thankfully, Tia's breasts were released.

"You, you lying Tutsi dog!" the Hutu rose to his feet and raced for the weapon he'd left on the chair.

A shot rang out. The Hutu sank to his knees, grabbed his gun and crawled to the tent opening where Bolongo had escaped. With an unearthly moan, he fell dead.

Overhead, she heard the dit-dit-dit of helicopter blades and wondered if things were getting better or worse.

Instinctively, Tia dropped to the ground. Spitting dirt, she wriggled closer to the chair on the opposite side of the room. She had to get out of there.

Tia managed to back up to the chair and retrieve the Hutu's knife. Suffering flashbacks of her flight from Uvira over a week ago, she struggled to put the blade to the ropes that bound her. Two slight nicks and an eternity later, she was free.

Running and shouting commenced all around the perimeter of her feeble shelter before she heard more shots.

"Hurry." She urged herself off the floor, ripping the rag from her mouth, spitting out the taste of dirt and male sweat.

She hoped the sudden silence meant all the men were preoccupied elsewhere. Sounds of distant gunfire sounded promising, but that could change at any moment.

Tia moved cautiously to the tent opening. Her toe struck in the Hutu commander inadvertently. His blood stained her shoes. He hadn't been a looker when he was alive. As a dead man, his ugliness took on a monsterish quality.

She could no longer hear the helicopters and wondered where they had gone. Had Leonard been telling the truth when he said troops were looking for her? Maybe the helicopters were her way out, maybe they had chased off the Hutus.

She ran into the bush, praying she would find the camp or someone familiar and not get lost forever in the wilderness.

It occurred to her that for the first time ever, she was alone. Truly alone. There was no one to help her now, her survival depended upon no one but herself.

Terror threatened to drop her on the spot. Forcing her feet to move, Tia refused to give in to it. She walked on the side of the path where matted grasses cushioned the sound of her footsteps as she'd seen Joseph do. She would find the camp on the border, find the helicopters or Joseph. She had to.

Joseph raced over the dead bodies in a crouch. David and the other two men scoured the perimeter. They'd heard gunfire traveling east and chanced coming inside the Hutu camp. He prayed he wouldn't find Tia dead in one of the Hutu tents.

The largest was peppered with holes. Joseph hesitated beside the dead Hutu commander's body, trying to prepare himself for the inevitable. He noted the indentation of a shoe near his body. It was too small to be a combat boot and the pattern looked more like a tire. It had to be Tia's.

Racing inside, he scanned the disheveled room. Near the cot the dirt looked as if someone had been crawling around in circles. Then, by the legs of a chair, he saw the discarded knife and the cut pieces of rope. She had to have been here.

He had to find her, she was probably terrified.

"Did you find anything?" a nervous Mason whispered from the tent opening.

"She was here." Joseph pushed past him. "I think she escaped from the Hutus."

"Where did she go, then?" Mason searched the push as if he expected to see her sitting and waiting for him.

Joseph thought for a moment. "Back to the border. That's the only place she would think she could find."

Within moments, he'd rounded up David and the others and was headed back to the refugee camp. He gave a silent prayer to the ancient spirits that he'd guessed right.

❖❖❖

Leonard ducked inside a huddle of bushes to catch his breath. He'd killed at least three Hutus back there. "How many's that? A dozen today?" Looking upward, he sought his father's response. He couldn't hear him speak from the spirit world, but Leonard knew he was close by.

His father had been beheaded two years ago and Leonard had vowed to avenge the old man's death. He hadn't gotten respect and approval while his father had lived, but he would now. Approval was showered upon him with every man he killed. He felt it.

"Did you see that, Sir?" The old man always insisted on being called "sir." He'd always liked British hierarchy and their love for titles. "That was a beaut of a slaughter wasn't it?"

Leonard laughed, but not too loud. Not because he was afraid of the few remaining Hutus, he assured himself. It would be nothing to finish them off. He just had to catch his breath first.

Remembering his empty gun clip, Leonard changed the empty one for full. Lovingly, he caressed the steel shaft. It was warm and smelled of spent gunpowder. An erotic smell, it was.

Dropping to the ground, he brought out his next favorite weapon. His knife, still flecked with Hutu blood, glinted in the waning light of day. He cleaned the blade on a patch of thick grass.

"You have to be ready, my babies," he spoke to the weapons as if they were, in fact, children. "After the Hutus, we've got an ex-Tutsi Commander to finish off."

He debated between killing Desiré or taking him back as a traitor. In Kigali, he'd sought out Laurent Kabila's assistant to tell him that Joseph had struck up allegiance with the Hutus. It was true, after all. Joseph had turned against the rebel cause, protecting Hutus. Amani said he would set a price on Joseph's head.

"If I take him back, he'll be hung." Leonard laughed delightedly. He wanted to be in the front row to watch him die.

Eight

"Tia knows med'sin. When she come back?" Denis asked his father, the seriousness in his eyes showed understanding beyond his years. He was fully aware of just how ill his mother was.

"I don't know, Denis." Fidele worried where Tia was and had sent two of his older sons to search the brush in case she'd lost her way. Weighing heavier on his heart was his wife's condition. He feared something was horribly wrong with Sarini. She had fallen ill late yesterday, and though he'd given her plenty of water from the nearby falls, she suffered from a high fever. The French woman, Nicole, believed she had the virus that was spreading around camp. She was kind when she spoke to him about her fears. Sarini, already exhausted, was sure to die soon if she didn't get antibiotics.

"We'll add Tia to our prayers," Fidele said to his son, caressing one of his soft cheeks. They'd been on their knees for the past hour, asking for Sarini's health to improve. Fidele didn't know what else to do.

A thrumming noise sounded in the far-off sky at that moment. It was the sound of hope. He knew aid workers would appear by air to drop off crates of food when they knew there was a need.

The helicopter landed in the empty clearing. No food crates were unloaded. Only U.N. soldiers spilled from the aircraft.

Fidele rose from his prayers and gathered around the newcomers with the rest of the disappointed but curious refugees. Why were they here if not to bring food?

An American soldier, clearly the person in charge, talked into a megaphone asking for anyone who was injured or sick. Fidele's heart lifted as he realized the helicopter would be used to transport the very ill to the hospital. He barely heard the rest of what the man had to say, but tucked away the information that soldiers would remain to escort the stronger refugees into Kigali.

Quickly, Fidele ran to get his wife. They would take her to the hospital. Sarini would be made well.

Denis ran at his side. "We did it!" he exclaimed. "Our pwayers worked!"

Fidele laughed, sharing in his son's elation. "That's right, Denis. They worked." He lifted Sarini from the ground so quickly, his daughter barely had time to remove the wet cloth from her mother's forehead. Nearly weightless in his arms, Sarini barely opened her eyes. "I do not want to leave you," she whispered hoarsely in French.

Fidele tucked her closer to his heart. "You must go," he said. "They will make you well in the hospital."

"No." her protest was so weak. "We must...stay together."

"Escusí, Monsieur." Fidele offered his wife to one of the soldiers at the opening of the helicopter. "My wife is very ill. Please take her."

"She'll be the last," the American officer stepped up. "We're at capacity now." he spoke to his men. "We'll have to come back for the rest."

Wails of protest and grief rose from the group of Hutus still arriving with sick family members. Fidele was grateful he'd made it back quickly, but terrified by the medic's grim demeanor as he loaded Sarini into the helicopter.

His dear wife now drifted somewhere between this world and the next where he could no longer reach her. Tired and hollow, her eyes looked through him as he placed a soft kiss on her dry, hot lips before he was asked to step back. She tasted of sickness and despair.

Fidele watched the aircraft until it disappeared into the perfect blue of the sky. He felt Denis at his side before the child spoke. "Mommy fly away."

"Yes." Fidele lifted the boy into his arms.

The remaining U.N. soldiers split rank. Some would stay to nurse the ill until the next helicopter transport arrived. The rest prepared to lead the healthy people inside Rwanda to their homes. Fidele gathered his children, then fell in step with the second group. As the Hutus and their armed escort began to walk, someone began singing. It was a song of hope, with an upbeat rhythm. Fidele lent his voice to the group and bounced Denis on his shoulders. They were going home.

Maneuvering around the arm of a dead man, Tia tried to avert her eyes from the bone littered path. Skin textured like rawhide clung stubbornly to some of the skeletal remains. Most were bare and stark white against the dark earth.

Don't think about it, Tia. She didn't want to know what had happened to these people, but suspected they'd been slaughtered trying to get past the Hutu militia.

Seeing the faded, tattered Mickey Mouse T-shirt molded to a child-sized ribcage brought her to her knees. When she and the other aid workers had come to Africa, they had brought T-shirts for the children. T-shirts with all kinds of cartoon characters on them. Denis had one, but refused to wear it. He'd only take it from his mother's basket to look at it for a while, then replace it, considering it too priceless to wear.

Tia sat heavily in the grass trying to stop the sickness in her empty stomach and the dizziness in her head. Swishing water from the confiscated Hutu canteen around her mouth, she rid herself of the acidic taste of bile burning the back of her throat.

Forcing herself forward, Tia took in the horror of the scene. The bodies spread for yards down the road, as if the refugees had been hunted down as they ran. The people who did this were worse than animals.

Averting her eyes, Tia looked toward the sky. Another helicopter, or perhaps the same one, passed overhead.

"Hey! Down here!" She jumped up and down trying to get their attention. The aircraft made steady progress away from her. "They can't see me." Tia was exhausted, near tears and ready to give up, when she heard the voices.

Tia moved to the side of the path and crept forward. She tried not to breath too hard, or make any other sound that would alert someone to her presence.

Leonard woke with a start, gripping his weapons tightly. Voices whispered on the late afternoon breeze, passing within inches of his leafy hideout. Fury ripped through his belly along with recognition. The Hutus failed to kill Desiré. But he would succeed.

Charging through the foliage of his shelter, Leonard screamed and came up behind the four Tutsis. Relieved to see Joseph without his panga, he rushed toward the surprised rebels. "Die, Desiré. Die!"

A series of rapidly fired shots from Leonard's gun sent Joseph's men flying onto their backs. He tossed his gun aside and barreled toward the last man standing.

Joseph dodged his would-be killer and grabbed Leonard's knife-wielding hand. Twisting his hip, he upended his ex-second-in-command and dropped him to the ground. Adrenaline raced through his veins, bunching his muscles taut as bowstrings. No more could he excuse the man's actions as grief for his family. Leonard Bolongo had to be stopped.

Straddling Leonard's powerfully compact body, Joseph struggled to free the cold steel from the man's iron grip. "Killing me won't make it better, Leonard."

Leonard grunted under Joseph's weight, but said nothing.

Pounding Leonard's fist against a rock, Joseph tried to force the weapon free. "The pain stays no matter how many Hutus die. Don't you understand?"

"Nooo!" Leonard shouted stubbornly. He held tighter to his knife, though his wounded knuckles bloodied the stone. "My father must be avenged."

Joseph's breathing became labored. Thighs strained to keep him upright as Leonard attempted to toss him over. "Then why kill me?"

For a moment, their eyes connected. Joseph read white-hot confusion mixed with red-ringed rage in his opponent's eyes. "I didn't kill your family." He could feel Leonard strain against his own thoughts. "And neither did those refugees you've killed. Where's your revenge?"

With an unearthly yell, Leonard heaved Joseph onto the ground. Closing both hands around the hilt of his

knife, he pushed all of his weight into a downward thrust.
The point came within a half inch of Joseph's throat, but
was kept from going further by the sheer strength of
Joseph's arm.

Cowards always fought hardest when it came time to
die, Leonard thought with disgust. "Don't try to reason
with me." Sweat poured from his face. His teeth ground
as he strained to force the knife into flesh. "You're too
soft to be commander. Kabila should have chosen me!"

Joseph's arms burned from holding the knife off his
neck. He was only a weak moment away from joining his
dead family in the spirit world. A vision of his mother
drifted past his eyes. Was it an invitation?

Leonard felt Joseph's hands begin to shake. Yeah. He
knew, it was only a matter of time.

Tia rounded the bend in the road with less caution. Shots
had been fired and men were shouting. Unless she was
going totally nuts, one of them was Joseph.

Her heart did a double-time march as stray light from
the setting sun spotlighted the struggling bodies of
Leonard and Joseph.

Leonard straddled Joseph, growling in rage as he
pushed a knife within a whisper of Joseph's throat. The
silver tip wavered dangerously as Joseph strained against
the full weight of the man above him.

Anger and urgency pushed Tia's fear aside. On pure instinct, she pulled the gun from her waist and raced down the road.

"Get off of him, Leonard!"

Both men registered surprise at her presence. The knife tip remained on target to kill.

"Stay there, my lovely." Leonard's voice fairly hissed with hate. "When I finish here, I'll take care of you."

His red-rimmed eyes and twisted grimace made Tia's blood run cold.

"Run, Tia," Joseph grunted. "I'm ready to die if the gods wish it."

"I'm not ready to give you up." She kept her gun trained on Leonard.

A renewed struggle began between the two men. "I mean it, Leonard. Get off him or I'll use this."

Joseph actually managed a half laugh. "Sh—She's a good shot. Remember?"

Leonard's eyes narrowed. He did remember. Tia could see him reconsidering.

Tia no more than blinked before Leonard cast back his arm to throw his knife at her. Everything moved slowly, including the bass-like pounding of Tia's pulse. Leonard's wild eyes went round as saucers. Joseph's deep voice thundered "No!" as he grabbed Leonard by the neck. Leonard released the jagged-edged weapon. Pocket-sized before, the weapon now loomed the size of Joseph's panga in her eyes.

Simultaneously, Tia squeezed a shot from her gun. Forgetting to brace herself, the kick of the gun knocked her backward. The knife whisked eerily past her eyes as she fell.

Her back hit the ground squarely, knocking the wind out of her and put the world back into real time. Too shocked to move, she lay studying the red-orange streaked sky. It was so beautiful. Why hadn't she noticed before?

"Tia." Joseph was above her. "Are you all right?"

He was beautiful. She had noticed that before. Smiling, she ran a hand down his dirt-powdered face. "I love you, Joseph."

The creases of concern were erased from his forehead as he released a magnificent smile. His thunderous laugh filled the air. "Are you sure, or does a near-death experience bring out your affections?"

"Tia. Oh my God." A shaken Mason appeared, dragging an automatic weapon.

Convinced she was going crazy, Tia thought her ex-husband an apparition. "Mason? Is it really you?"

"Yes," Mason replied. "I ran into Desiré here while I was selling weapons. I asked to come along when he said he was looking for you."

"I knew you would find me." She turned to Joseph.

"It's become my life's work." He smiled and helped her to her feet, but kept a firm grip on her hands.

Tia could now see Leonard sprawled on the ground directly in front of her. A hole, centered perfectly on his forehead, oozed crimson liquid. "Am I dreaming?" she asked.

Joseph held her close. "I'm afraid not."

The world whirled around her. "I killed Leonard." Her knees gave way as the full impact of her actions filled her conscious thoughts. "I killed him."

Joseph pulled her into his arms to keep her from falling.

"I'm a murderer." Her voice was barely a whisper. She hated saying the words, and hated more the way they sounded.

"You're not a murderer," Joseph spoke over her head, steadying her shaking body. "If you hadn't shot him, I'd be dead. Would you prefer that?"

Mason wandered in a dazed circle, muttering something about how amazing her shot was, but that wasn't what she needed to hear. She'd taken a man's life. And though Leonard was the devil's own, she was sickened to know she'd stooped to his level.

"I came here to help people. Not kill them." Her lips quivered as the horror of her act intensified.

"It's all right, Tia." Joseph's soft tone and massaging hands on her back helped soothe her jangled nerves. "If you can grieve for taking a man's life, it means you're still human. It's only when you stop trying to feel..." She heard him swallow hard.

His hand traveled down her arm to her hand. Until that moment, she hadn't realized that she still held the weapon. Joseph's warm hand closed over hers and eased the gun from her numb fingers and let it fall to the ground.

"You saved my life." He kissed her forehead with divine tenderness. "And I'm happier than I thought I could be."

A laugh rumbled in his chest. Tia liked the way it mixed with his steady heartbeat.

"For the first time in years," he continued, "I'd rather live than die."

"I'm glad you're alive." Tia couldn't imagine living through this African nightmare without him. How could she leave when all she wanted was to be with this man? Without warning, all the tensions, fears and frustrations of the past two weeks welled up inside Tia. She buried her face in Joseph's torn shirt and cried. What would she do about loving this man?

Joseph held tight to the only woman he'd ever loved as she sobbed. Gently, he kissed the explosion of raven curls on top of her head, grateful for another chance to touch her.

As the last bit of sunlight dipped below the horizon, he decided that these could not be his final moments with Tia. She didn't belong in Africa. She was much too frail for the violence of his land. But his heart remained selfishly stubborn. He had to keep her here. She was everything he needed. All the reason to live he could ever dream of.

Mason had begun to assist two of his men whom Joseph had thought dead. Quickly, Joseph sent thanks to the spirit for sparing their lives—and his own.

Pushing away, Tia wiped at the tears on her face. "You'd better go help your men."

"You sure you're okay?" He didn't tell her he planned to hold her for the rest of her life. A thousand lifetimes.

She nodded and walked away to find a seat on a large stump. It tore at him to see the lost expression she wore.

As darkness fell, Fidele could feel his steps grow heavy. An uneasiness crept up his spine as he noticed the two U.N. soldiers working their way back in the crowd as his fellow Hutus pointed behind them.

A familiar scent of wildflowers that had been uniquely Sarini's swirled fragrantly in the air about him. It was a beautiful, warm feeling—mystical. A closeness so wonderful, Fidele wept.

Sarini spoke to him, telling him she was all right—but that she wouldn't be waiting when he arrived in Kigali. His precious Sarini was leaving this world, beginning a new life in the next...without him.

Shuddering with grief, Fidele continued walking, dropping tears to the hard, packed earth. Denis lay his head back on his father's shoulder. He began patting his father's back. His children moved closer to him, yet he felt lonely.

"Monsieur Zavi?" One of the soldiers was beside him now.

"Oui." Fidele already knew why the man's face was so solemn.

"We regret to inform you that your wife was dead when she reached the hospital. We are sorry."

Fidele nodded his understanding. "*Merci.*"

Fidele kept moving when the soldiers walked ahead, knowing that if he stopped, he'd never be able to continue. Looking up toward the sky, he thought he saw a beam of light that lit the blue sky beneath it. He ached to touch her one last time, to see love in her soft brown eyes. With envy, he said to the spirit, "Take care of her. Please, take care of her."

Steadying his wobbling legs, he continued down the path to Kigali. It was up to him to raise their children alone. To see them safe and hope for a better life for each of them. It was Sarini's dream as well. He couldn't let her down.

Tia couldn't squeeze out another tear. And she was too tired to try. The U.N. troop and refugees had found them as they walked toward Kigali. The news of Sarini's death had taken Tia into a deeper depression. A deeper level of grief. Wearily, she rocked Denis in her arms, though he'd fallen asleep long before. Somehow, it made her feel closer to her friend to hold her youngest child.

Mason and Joseph had asked alternately during the evening if she needed anything. She'd refused and kept rocking.

The U.N. soldiers had tended to Joseph's wounded men and now hung on the fringes of the bonfire, respectfully quiet as a solemn wake ensued.

Fidele, his children and the other refugees sat humming and singing mournfully around a large fire. In turn, each refugee wished their sister, Sarini, a safe journey to the next world.

As the last of the Hutus gave their well wishes, Joseph moved forward.

Surprise shown clearly on Fidele's face as the Tutsi held his arms out and turned his face skyward. The drumming and soft singing continued as this Hutu enemy kneeled before the sacred fire.

Mason leaned to whisper at Tia, "What's this, some kind of pagan ritual?"

"Shh!" Tia shushed him irritably. She watched the yellow glow of the fire flicker over Joseph's magnificent African god-like physique.

Taking a handful of ashes, Joseph smeared the gray powder over his gleaming bare chest, then his face. Raising a rock to the sky, he spoke to the spirit in a strange dialect. His native tongue, Tia suspected.

Listening carefully, she managed to understand some of what he said. Enough to know he wished Sarini a good trip to the spirit world and that any bad deeds she'd committed should be brought to bear upon the rock he held, not her.

Tia was touched beyond words by his sincerity and heartfelt sentiments. He ended his short, powerful speech with the wish for peace between the warring tribes.

All fell silent as he sought Fidele's attention. Hand on the smaller man's shoulder, he spoke in French so that everyone could understand. "I've watched you with your wife, Monsieur Zavi. The sweet looks that passed between you, the tenderness as you touched her arm or hand."

He glanced at Tia before speaking again. "Only now do I begin to understand the depth of the love you must've felt for her." His dark eyes held Tia's for a moment before returning to Fidele.

Fidele's eyes glistened with emotion.

Tia heard Mason shift and sigh impatiently beside her.

Joseph continued, "I want you to know that I'm sorry for your loss. Sorry for this war and any part I had in putting your family in this position."

Fidele sat straighter. "Don't apologize, my friend. We Hutus were at fault for killing hundreds and thousands of your people, weren't we?"

Joseph hung his head. "True. But we retaliated. Neither of our tribes has gained from the killing."

"No." Fidele stood and stared deep into the yellow and orange flames. "No one wins."

"Agreed." Joseph stood. He towered over the Hutu man, but offered a hand in friendship. "You have my word that I will do whatever I can to bring peace to the countries of Rwanda and Zaire."

The two men's hands slapped together in truce.

Fidele tightened his grip and offered a sad smile. Moving to stand before Tia, the man gave a glance at his sleeping son. "You'll be leaving soon, Tia."

She gave a single nod.

"I'm not sure how Denis will survive without your fairy tales each day."

"They aren't fairy tales. They're true stories."

Fidele looked askance. "Not to us."

"This war is ridiculous." Tia laid the child on her blanket. "All it's accomplishing is getting the nations of Hutus and Tutsis killed."

"Maybe it will be different with a new leader."

"What makes you think the rebel leader will do anything more for you than President Habyarimana or Mboto has these past couple of decades?"

"With the exception of Leonard Bolongo, we've been treated better by these Tutsis than our own Hutu militia," Fidele argued, gesturing toward Joseph. "At least Joseph Desiré sees us as people."

That much was true. Tia had to concede that Joseph, no matter how humorless, had treated the Hutu men as equals throughout their journey. He'd consulted them when the path seemed to disappear or fork in too many directions. He'd had his men help the older folks when their burdens had grown heavy.

"Joseph himself is different." She looked toward the man, a towering figure against the flickering light of the fire. "But, it'll be pure luck if Joseph's leader turns out to be anything but another money-hungry dictator," she said.

Fidele shrugged. "We'll hope for the best."

"Why hope? Why not do something?" Tia's exasperation returned. "The whole lot of you should storm Zaire and Rwanda's capital cities and demand governments for the people."

Fidele scoffed. "And should we run before bullets to make certain we die, as well?"

"It's better than what you're doing now."

Fidele gave her a warning scowl. "What's that?"

"Running between raindrops believing you'll stay dry." She hadn't meant to raise her voice, but couldn't seem to help it. "Eventually this war will soak you with death, Fidele."

"If I risk my life, who'll look after my family?"

Tia placed her hands on the man's slim shoulders. "So, what if you keep them alive, Fidele? What then? Poverty and starvation aren't much to look forward to."

Fidele looked stricken. "You have no right to judge me." With narrowed eyes and a tortured expression, he scanned the sleeping forms of his numerous children with a face that suddenly looked older than his years. "I've always hoped for change. Hoped that when my children were adults, things would be different. Yet Emmanuel will soon be eighteen. A man. Nothing has changed for the better."

Tia, surprised by his unusual show of temper, stepped back. She'd put her foot too far down her own throat to breathe.

"Every day I have to ask myself 'will we run again?'" Fidele strode in wide circles, his arms gesturing broadly. His children began to wake then. "I pushed my wife though she was tired and weak. I wanted her to escape the bullets. To survive this war." Tears nearly poured from the man's eyes. "I know I pushed her, but I had no choice."

"Of course you didn't, Fidele." Tia wanted to go to him and make up for her words, but it was too late. Fidele kept circling and ranting.

"And if we don't get home and rebuild our city, will this be the day the rest of my family dies?" Stopping, his eyes wandered the awakening children, slowly he brought his arms down to his side, then bent to caress his youngest son's head. "Denis has never seen our home—doesn't know what it's like to have solid walls around him."

"I know," Tia sniffed and took a tentative step in his direction. "But he has you to love him."

"Yes. A father you call a coward." His look was convicting.

Shaking her head, Tia struggled to find an apology. "I didn't mean it, Fidele. Honest."

"I refuse to abandon my children, Tia." His coal black eyes were fierce and bright. "They need me with them today and every day. It may be years before things improve for the people of Rwanda and Zaire. I want my children to know that I loved them enough to make each day as comfortable as possible—that I fought the battle of starvation and illness with them. Now is when they need me most!"

One knee to the ground, a hand to his child's head and his adoring family looking on, Fidele was all a man should be.

Profoundly humbled, Tia sank to the ground and offered her hand to him. Words weren't enough to show how sorry she was.

Her extended arm wavered in the gusty air as she waited. Then, as quickly as it had come, Fidele's anger diminished. Fidele grasped her hand and pulled her into a tight hug. Shaking with sobs, he poured his anger out in tears.

You're a good father," she whispered. "I was out of line. I'm just so upset about Sarini. Please...say we're still friends."

Fidele placed a hand on Tia's head.

He said nothing, but Tia knew she'd been forgiven. Relief nearly made her cry all over again. How could she be so stupid as to almost throw away the best friend she'd ever had?

Mason took the momentary silence as an opportunity to speak, "You know who always wins in a war?"

Tia eyed him curiously as she and Fidele parted.

"The arms dealers," he continued on, without encouragement.

"That's why you're here, right?" Tia knew he frequently traveled to Africa on business. What kind she hadn't known until today.

"Partially," he granted. "Since I know my way around central Africa pretty well, I volunteered to escort your parents here. They're waiting at the embassy in Kinshasa, Zaire, hoping you turn up alive.

"My parents are in Africa?" Tia missed them both dearly.

Mason nodded, his aristocratically handsome features lit by the flames of the fire. "When Desiré told me you'd probably be headed back toward the border, I had one of my men contact the embassy to let them know. It's not a coincidence that the U.N. troops found your new friends."

"You arranged that too?"

"No." This time the American U.N. officer spoke across the flames. "Your mother contacted the U.N. Secretary and requested our assistance when the Tutsi rebel, Bolongo, came to claim the money for your return."

Tia was confused. "Why would my parents give him reward money if they hadn't found me?"

The officer scowled. "He wouldn't say a word without getting the money first. They gambled he was telling the truth and asked that we follow him."

"My point is ..." Mason took back the conversation. "You could all be wealthy men, Tutsis and Hutus alike, if you work with me."

Tia shouldn't have been surprised at this self-serving offer. It was so typically Mason. "What are you talking about, Mason?"

"Desiré, we should form a partnership." He sought Joseph's attention. "You have connections with the rebel leader, he needs guns. Together we'll strike a deal to be his exclusive supplier."

"I just struck a truce with the Hutus." Joseph said incredulously. "How can I sell your arms?"

"I didn't say you had to use them," Mason countered. "And you, Zavi. You and your friends can deliver arms to the Hutu militia in remote areas for me."

Fidele gave an angry reply and turned his back on Mason.

Tia rose to her feet completely livid. "Didn't you see all those dead bodies on our way here, Mason?"

"What's that to do with me?" he asked.

"Guns did that, you idiot."

"Tia, you surprise me." Mason grinned and found his dented cigarette case. "You know what they say back home. Guns don't kill people. People kill people. At least that's the way it looked when you plugged that Tutsi rebel earlier."

It was a cruel thing to say. Tia felt renewed guilt punch her in the gut like a fist. Suddenly ill, she took refuge in the nearby bush.

Angry, Joseph knelt down to look Mason directly in the eye. "I don't need guns. Nor do I need the kind of wealth you have. I can see why she left you."

"I left her," Mason shouted after Joseph's retreating back. "Don't believe any lies she may have told you."

Nine

Joseph followed Tia as she'd run into the brush and found her sobbing uncontrollably on the ground. Once again, he took her and held her.

"I can't believe he hates me enough to come all the way here to add further torment to my life." She wiped her eyes.

"I think he's still in love with you," Joseph said honestly. He'd watched the man panic when he thought Tia was in danger. How he'd rushed to her side when she'd fallen to the ground.

"Don't be silly, Joseph. That man has done nothing but make my life a living hell since before our divorce." Her sobbing diminished as she found the hate she'd designated just for Mason Algood.

"Divorce?" Joseph was relieved. He wasn't certain if the marriage had been dissolved. "I can't imagine how a man could be such a fool."

Tia sat silently for a while. "He had his reasons," she finally said in a quiet voice.

Sensing she didn't want to pursue the subject, Joseph let it drop.

"This is beginning to be a habit," Joseph smiled. "You and me, in the middle of the night."

"Yeah." Tia gave a slight chuckle. "It's a nice night," she said gazing at the sky.

"Would you like me to tell you a story?" he asked.

Tia looked at him quizzically. The full moon lit her face like an angel's. "You? Tell me a story?"

"Mmm-hmm. Like you tell the children. It may help you sleep."

Shifting in his lap, she frowned. "I doubt that I'll ever get a good night's sleep again. But, go ahead."

"There once was a mean Tutsi rebel, hell-bent on revenge."

"Hah." Tia laughed then. "I think I've heard this one."

"You're interrupting," Joseph chided with a crooked grin.

"Sorry. Continue."

"One day the rebel grew tired of killing. And he cried to his dead mother , 'Will I never kill enough to avenge you?' Now, his mother was a wise spirit who looked down upon her heartbroken son and whispered in his ear. 'The truth is coming. The truth will be enough.'"

He looked deeply into Tia's eyes as he continued, not wanting her to miss the meaning of his story, his heart pounding as he lifted all pretenses and shields of his true feelings. "The next day, the rebel heard the cries of a woman in distress. Without thinking, he raced toward her voice and found her hanging from the side of a steep mountain."

Tia's breath caught in her throat. She sat up straighter, moving to the ground beside him.

Holding her hands, Joseph sat opposite her, his heart thundering like a herd of cape buffalo. "The rebel saved the woman and promised to see her safely home. He didn't know that along the way, the woman would tell him the truth." He paused to watch her reaction.

She didn't move, just squeezed his hands tighter.

"The truth was there would never be satisfaction in killing. Only in building. Building a new country, making friends of enemies, protecting the children from a future of doom."

Her head dropped then. Joseph saw two bright teardrops fall to the ground in the moonlight.

Kissing her hands, he waited for the lump in his throat to subside. "The rebel decided to change what he fought for. He would find a way to end the war, to rebuild his country. True to his word, he led the woman safely home, though he didn't want her..." his voice broke, "didn't want her to go."

Tia threw her arms around his neck and held him so tight he didn't think he could breathe.

Swallowing back his own emotion, Joseph laid her on her back and gazed into the soft brown eyes that he'd learned to love. "The rebel not only discovered the truth, but that in saving the woman, he'd actually saved himself."

Tia pulled him down to kiss him. "Thank you, Joseph. That was a lovely story."

"Ready to go back?" he asked, not really wanting to share her with anyone else.

"In a minute." Tia closed her eyes and put her hands behind her head. "It's peaceful here. Let's enjoy it a while longer."

Happiness filled Joseph. He stretched out beside her on the ground, perfectly content to remain as long as she wished.

Mercifully, Kigali was only three miles from where they'd stopped the previous night. Tia hadn't slept well despite Joseph's best effort to the contrary. His story played over in her mind as they walked, however, and she looked at him from time to time. He stayed by her side the entire journey.

Mason spoke with one of the U.N. soldiers. Judging from his awkward gait, his feet were killing him. Tia took pity on him and his expensive leather loafers. Definitely the wrong kind of shoes for strolling the jungle. If not for the sandals Joseph had fashioned for her from old tire and jungle vines, she wouldn't have made it out of the misty mountains.

It was silly, she knew, to be sentimental about the unfashionable footwear, but Joseph had made them for her. She'd pack them as her only souvenirs of Africa.

A twang of regret filled her. She'd come to care so much for these people. For Fidele and his family. For Joseph.

Tia had fallen in love with him as swiftly as her slide from the mountain path. When he'd kissed her, there was no world outside his arms and, perhaps, that's why she walked with heavy steps today. He'd said last night he didn't want her to go. If only she could stay. If only she'd told him the real truth.

As if reading her mind, Mason fell into step beside her, one of his sharp grins playing on his face. "I tried to send you a telegram when I heard you were here."

Tia sighed. "I can't believe you're bringing this up."

"You got it then? Kid looks just like his dad."

"I'm sure he's a beautiful baby, Mason. Congratulations." She said it, but didn't feel it.

He ran a hand through his wavy hair. "Cynthia can't wait to have another."

She held up a hand. "I get it, okay?"

"Get what?" His mock surprise was almost believable.

"You know what. Now let it go." Old hurt and anger boiled to the surface. "Before I tell you the thousand ways you can go to hell."

Authentic surprise lit his face. Taking a step back, Mason shook his head. "You've changed, Tia."

This was the first time she'd spoken face-to-face with him since the divorce. It was satisfying to tell him what she thought without benefit of a lawyer filtering her words. "Sorry if I offended you," she said without an ounce of remorse. "Being on the run through the jungles for the past week has lowered my tolerance for your bull."

"My bull?"

Seeing the argument coming, Tia held up a finger. "Not now, Mason. I'm anxious to help my friends, see my parents and get out of these clothes. I've been in them for a week."

"I could've guessed from the smell." Mason's nose wrinkled.

Walk away, Tia. Just walk away.

With great effort, she managed to turn away from his insult and move toward Joseph. Tia couldn't believe her luck could get any worse, but when the only person from the entire continent of America she doesn't want to see shows up in the middle of war-torn Africa, the pits of hell couldn't be far off.

Joseph listened to the interaction with interest. He was certain Mason still loved her. Why then did he intentionally rile her? Tia approached. He lifted an eyebrow. "Nice man, your ex."

"I'd rather not talk about it," she said, angrily.

"I take it he is well liked in America?" Joseph couldn't help but tease her about her odd choice in husbands.

Tia rolled her eyes. "He's charismatic, good-looking and makes tons of money. People choose to ignore his shortcomings."

"Ah, money." Joseph nodded. "Seems men will do anything to obtain it."

"Mason will."

They reached the hotel in Kigali an hour and twenty minutes later.

Joseph turned to Tia. "My men and I will stay here. You could stay," he said tentatively. "Call the Kinshasa Embassy."

"I need to find my parents. show them I'm all right."

She was putting him off. Joseph could feel panic rise.

"We'll make sure she gets there all right." It was one of their U.N. escorts. "Her parents are anxious to see her."

Tia looked up at the man she loved. "You kept your end of the bargain, Joseph. You've seen me safely home. Thank you again, for everything."

Joseph watched her go. His heart couldn't hurt worse if Leonard's knife were there to cut it in two. "Wait." He couldn't bear her leaving.

She turned.

"I have one question."

"Yes?" She looked fearful of what he would ask.

"If you could choose to go back to America or do something fulfilling here in Zaire, which would you choose?"

Tears welled in her eyes as Tia shook her head. "There's no right answer to that question, Joseph. Please don't ask me."

"Why not?"

"I've already made my choice." With that she walked off.

"Women, eh?" Mason shrugged. "Listen, maybe later we could talk about an introduction to Laurent Kabila."

Joseph turned and headed for the hotel lobby to keep from choking Mason on the spot. Once inside, Joseph leaned over the front desk. "I need a phone," he demanded of the desk clerk. "Now!"

Unnerved by the sight of the angry Tutsi, the slight man ran a nervous hand over his bald head. "Right away, sir." He reached beneath his counter and produced the item and queried with hopeful eyes, "Will you be needing a room?"

Joseph studied the man a moment, then nodded. "I didn't mean to be rude," he said by way of apology. "I'll be needing three rooms for myself and my men," he added in a more civilized tone. He had two men airlifted to the hospital and the rest were dead, thanks to Bolongo.

Instantly appeased, the clerk began collecting keys and punching numbers on an antiquated computer.

Joseph went back to the phone, stabbing at the buttons. He huffed impatiently while the phone rang. "Amani," Joseph demanded when the connection went through, "we need to meet. How's tomorrow morning at eight?"

"Eight will be fine," Amani replied, "though I'm surprised you're so bold as to come here."

Joseph looked into the phone as if it could tell him what Amani had meant by his last remark. It didn't matter. He had to get some rest before the meeting.

Tia was extremely disappointed to find her parents had left the embassy. "Are you sure?" she asked the clerk again as she looked across the Jeep at the U.N. soldier driving.

"They're on their way to Kigali to see you, Ms. Algood," the sweet-voiced receptionist explained.

"Can't someone get hold of them and tell them I'm on my way there?"

"I'm afraid their plane has already taken off."

"I see. Thank you." She hung up the cellular phone and handed it to Mason who was in the back seat. "They're on their way to Kigali," she said to the driver. "Could you take me back to the hotel?"

Mason stopped rubbing his feet long enough to tuck away his phone. "Just as well. I'm dead tired." He struggled back into his shoes when they reached the hotel where they'd left Joseph and his men.

At the door, Tia froze. "I...I need some clean clothes. Do you have any money, Mason?"

"What kind of question is that?" Mason was happy to lift a couple of hundreds from his wallet and give them to her. "Tell you what, you don't have to pay that back."

"Thanks." Tia nearly ran down the soldiers outside the door in her haste.

The knock on the door irritated Joseph. He was just preparing for a shower. "Yes?" he yelled through the closed door.

"It's me." Tia held tight to her bag. It held a change of clothes, a comb, brush, toothpaste and toothbrush. "Can I tal—"

The door nearly flew off its hinges Joseph pulled it open so fast. "Tia.." He couldn't say more.

"My parents are coming here. I need somewhere to sleep..."

"Come in. Come in." Joseph gave a brilliant grin and stepped back from the doorway.

"Don't get too excited," Tia cautioned as she moved inside the room. If I stay, it's only for tonight. No complications, okay?"

"Right. No complications," Joseph agreed. He watched hungrily as she crossed the room to his bed.

Tia walked around the bed before sitting down. "What were you doing?"

Joseph realized he stood dressed only in his pants. "I was about to shower. Nothing important," he added quickly.

Tia's eyelids dropped seductively. "Did you know you have the most amazing physique I've ever seen?"

"Do I?" Joseph kneeled in front of her and placed her hands on his chest, over his heart. "Feel that?"

"Yes," Tia said in a low, husky tone.

"It's been doing that since the day I first saw you."

"That's the sweetest thing anyone's ever said to me."

"Easy to believe if the only man you've been around is Mason."

"Let's not talk about my ex-husband, okay? He's ruined my life enough."

"He was just the wrong man."

Tia was pretty sure she knew where this conversation was headed. She wanted no part of it. "I'm not talking about it, Joseph. No complications, remember?"

Sighing, Joseph planted a kiss on her neck. "I'm desperate enough to take you up on that."

Tia didn't want to talk about Mason or anything else. She just wanted to enjoy being lost in the moment. Joseph's hands were sliding up her legs, just under her shorts, then back down again.

Strong hands, Tia noted. When his lips touched her neck she could think of nothing but her long-suffering desire. Joseph laid her back on the bed and settled on top of her.

"Wait," she pushed him away gently. "I've got to shower. I look a fright and probably smell worse."

"You're kidding, right?" he asked breathlessly.

"No." She proceeded toward the bathroom.

With some effort, Joseph managed a normal voice. "You smell fine to me," he insisted, hoping she'd reconsider.

"That's sweet," she said. "Even if it's not true."

When her back was turned, he adjusted himself in hopes of finding some comfort. After their trek through the jungle with no toiletries he was no doubt smelling rather gamey himself. Not that it mattered to him. But women were funny that way. "Fine. I'll take one next." He didn't want to give her an excuse to turn him away.

Tia stood in the doorway of the bathroom for a moment. "You know," she paused, "we'll waste less water if you join me."

He couldn't control the grin that spread across his face or the speed with which he was inside the small room with her.

Her hands shook as she worked at the button and zipper of her shorts. Yanking carelessly at his own shorts, he stood nude in a matter of seconds.

Tia, looking as delicious as a bakery confection in her dirt-smudged flowered underwear, stood eyes wide and devouring. Joseph could drill for diamonds with his new level of arousal. An approving smile lifted her lips. "Are

you sure you can make it this far in your condition?"
Humor danced across her face.

Feeling carefree and playful for the first time in forever, Joseph crossed the floor in a step and enclosed her in
his arms. In one swift move, he unclasped her bra. With
another, her panties were around her ankles. "You'd be
amazed at what I can do in this condition."

This time when he kissed her, he did a thorough job
of it. Having her flesh against his flesh was more than
exciting. It was pure heaven. It occurred to him that he
should be gentle, but there was too much blood raging
through his veins for the patience it would require. If this
was his one and only chance to be with her, then every second counted.

Without taking his mouth from Tia's, he reached
behind her to start the water in the shower. The sooner
they were clean, the sooner he'd get what he craved.

Tia vowed never to forget this feeling. Joseph's soapy, sexy
massage and the hard spray of water against her sensitive
skin were more pleasure than she'd thought legal.

They explored each other's bodies and Tia reveled in
each new discovery. Joseph's long lean muscles were so
radically different from Mason's gymnasium-pumped pecs
that she ran her hands over them time and again. First,
running bubbles along the wide expanse of the chest she'd
been dying to touch, then plunging down the chiseled
bricks of his stomach.

He moaned and called her name. The walls magnified his deep baritone and made her feel more feminine than she had in years.

Fumbling with the small bottle of hotel shampoo, Tia attempted to washed her hair. Twice she dropped her hands and the bottle to lay her head back in ecstasy as Joseph fondled and suckled her breasts. Finally, he turned her and finished lathering her hair himself.

"We'll be prunes waiting on you to finish," he scolded good-naturedly. When he was done and there was no part of either of them still covered in soap, he lifted her from the shower and placed her on the cracked tile.

Drying off was another heavenly experience, topped off by Joseph's patiently combing through Tia's tangled curls while she sat nude on the bed. It was a hot night and she enjoyed the cool feeling of her damp hair on her back as he gently pulled the comb through each section. "Interesting way you have of seducing a woman, Desiré." She moaned with sheer delight.

His fingers slid down the slick strands of her hair onto her bare back. "I dreamed of you once," he said quietly.

Flattered, Tia let him talk. "Did you?"

"More than once, truthfully." Joseph pulled her hair from her face to lay it sideways across her back. "But the first dream was of you combing your hair with your fingers by that stream."

Moved, Tia turned to look at him. "That was no dream. I actually did that—right before I sat on you," she added with a twisted grin.

"And I tried to kill you." Joseph laughed and pushed her onto her back. "Until I felt these."

Tia arched and moaned as he massaged her breasts until the tips hardened. "Good thing I'm not flat-chested, huh?"

Joseph hummed his agreement as he nuzzled the valley between them. "Or you'd be dead."

Her laugh died under the heat of his assault of kisses. Suddenly, all playfulness was gone. Joseph's hands groped and kneaded. His kisses became more urgent, demanding. He pulled her legs apart and positioned himself between them.

Tia's lazy warmth turned to a hot drumming. Her body called for him. Moved to the rhythm of his dance of desire.

He was exquisitely impatient, passionately skilled in making her body sing beneath him.

Joseph made her feel free, wonderful, wanted. He called her name and she reveled in his wild lovemaking.

"Don't let this end. Don't let this end," she chanted, lost in ecstasy and never wanting to be found.

Ten

Somewhere between midnight and dawn, things became extremely complicated for Joseph. He'd had no intention of making love to Tia this one night and then allowing her to go.

Pulling her closer, her back to his chest, her soft bottom nestling perfectly against him, he closed his eyes and breathed deeply. She smelled like soap, shampoo, woman and sex. Hell, he couldn't stand her being on the other side of the bed, let alone the world.

He wanted her again. Wanted her to stay.

Kissing her neck and shoulders, he attempted to wake her up. Need burned again, more intense than before. "Tia," he whispered in her ear before nipping the lobe.

Tia rolled onto her back lazily, her eyes heavy with sleep. "You going for some kind of world record, Desiré?"

"No," he replied simply. "I just need you."

"Oh." She smiled and pushed him onto his back. "I'll see if I can take care of that for you."

She straddled him and Joseph felt a tremor of excitement. He grabbed her hips and kept her from moving.

"What?" she asked.

His emotions were too close to the surface. The words came out before he thought about it. "Stay with me."

Tia giggled and gave him a playful kiss. "I am with you, silly."

"No." He pushed up to a sitting position with her still on his lap. Smoothing her hair back, nuzzling her breasts with his face, he closed his eyes and prayed that this one time he got what he wanted. "I mean, stay here in Rwanda with me. Be my wife."

Her body froze. He could feel her heart begin a panicked rhythm against his cheek.

"Oh my God, Joseph." She pulled back. "You can't mean that."

"I do." Joseph sought her eyes. In them, he saw fear, but he didn't blame her for that. She'd be crazy not to be afraid of staying in the midst of a war. "You were right about me. I haven't allowed myself to feel anything but anger since my family died. It's kept more painful feelings away. Killing made me think I was avenging the loss of the most important part of my life."

She trembled now. Sympathy accompanied her tender strokes down his face. "I'm so sorry."

Joseph shook his head and struggled to find the words to help her understand how much he needed her. "I'm no prince. Not a rich man. I know you're used to having nice things." His words came faster now, tumbling out with unleashed emotion. "I'm going to ask for a job with the new government, today. Soon, I'll have money to take care of you."

"Oh, Joseph, I don't care about money." She moved off him and bounced onto the bed.

"Only because you've never been without it." Missing her touch, Joseph hooked an arm around her waist so she would go no further. "You and I can dedicate our lives to building a new Africa. I'll help run the government, you can organize schools, find funding for new farms and mining."

Fear changed to panic in her eyes. "Joseph, that's a lot of work, I don't think I'm up to the challenge."

"Of course you are. You're the first aid worker I've met who really wanted to help the refugees beyond throwing food at them like they were caged animals. Stand up and fight as you challenged Fidele to do."

She turned away. "The Zavis got me out of Uvira, you made certain I reached Rwanda alive. I've done nothing but be a burden to people who don't need any more."

"You've given these people hope, Tia." He took her cheek in his hand and urged her to look at him. "The stories you tell the children about America give them dreams and ideas of what they want their future to be. You lift everyone's spirits and don't allow them to give up."

"I didn't think you were listening." Her eyes were wide with surprise.

He'd been listening. And somehow her words had reached beyond the nails of his emotional coffin and released the love he'd buried within.

"When I first saw you, Tia, struggling along that mountain path, feet aching, exhausted, but still walking. A great darkness lifted from my heart. Because here, I thought, was true courage."

"I was scared of everything," she said with a laugh. "Of snakes, of bullets, of never getting down that mountain alive."

"But you didn't give up," Joseph insisted. "When you fell, I had to go down that mountain after you. Because only by saving you, could I save myself, remember?" Pausing, he let the importance of his words to sink in. "And now that I finally have something to live for, I don't want to lose it."

She trembled as he buried her lips beneath a kiss. Nothing had ever tasted as sweet. Joseph explored deeper with his tongue, encouraged by her fiery response.

Tia cried out his name as he covered her with kisses. Asked for him as he hardened in need once more. Then she began to push him away. "No. This is all wrong," she offered in a tortured voice. "Joseph, I can't marry you." She barely managed to get it out.

"Don't say no, Tia." He grasped her face firmly. "I know I'm asking a lot, for you to give up everything, but think about it."

"You don't understa—"

"Please," he insisted.

"I can't marry you, Joseph. It wouldn't be fair." Tia tucked her shirt into her jeans and watched anger and confusion play on his face.

"What's fair got to do with it? You love me, don't you?" he demanded. "Don't you?"

"Yes." Tia wanted to cry for the truth of it. She'd never loved Mason as much as this. Quite possibly, she'd never love anyone to the degree she loved this man. "I love you and that's why I can't punish you by marrying me."

"Punish . . ? What are you talking about?"

"I can't have children, Joseph." There. She'd said it.

Joseph looked at her as if stricken. "You can't?"

Shaking her head, Tia looked to the ground. "That's why Mason cheated on me. He wanted a child. And now he has one." Suddenly, her legs felt weak. She sank to the ground.

Joseph kneeled in front of her and lifted her chin. "It doesn't matter to me, Tia. I love you and I want to marry you."

Tears crowded her eyes. She could see how much he believed what he was saying. But she knew it wouldn't last. "Thank you, Joseph. Really. I know you mean what you say, but you'll change your mind. Just like Mason did."

"I'm not Mason." Fury raged once again. "Don't judge me as if I'd behave the same way."

"Honestly, Joseph, I'm not judging you." It was her turn to get angry. "It's fact. And even more so in

Rwanda. A man is no man without heirs. Tell me I'm wrong," she challenged.

"Of course, all men want sons. Lots of them. But look at my country, Tia. It's filled with war and hate. If I can't help bring about peace and a better government, what legacy would I have to give my children? It's better that I don't have any sons to be killed."

"That's a wonderful rationalization, but you don't mean it."

"Now, you're telling me what I mean?" he yelled.

"This country is about family. It's about rejoicing and working and grieving together as one unit. This war you've fought for two years is about family. It's so important to you, Joseph, that you've killed for it. Don't pretend now that it doesn't matter." Tia rose and started for the door.

"Wait. Where are you going?"

"Back where I belong." Sniffing, she put a hand on the doorknob.

Joseph covered her hand with his own. "Don't leave." He turned her around gently. "Is it so easy for you to dismiss my love?"

Tia couldn't stop the tears that spilled from her eyes. "No. Nothing's been easy since I met you. I love you, too, Joseph."

"Then don't leave. At least think about my proposal."

"All right," she agreed, because she no longer had the strength to resist. "I'll think about it."

"Thank you," he whispered. His first kiss was soft as a sigh before becoming more urgent and needy.

Tia allowed herself to get lost in the wonder of his lovemaking once again. Relishing every delicious caress of his skilled hands, she let him soothe her conscience and free her mind. If this was the last time he touched her—the last time he loved her—she wanted to enjoy every heart-stopping, delectable second.

Tangled moans of pleasure stopped Mason's knuckles a scant beat before knocking on the door. It was like listening to a porno film.

Anger hot enough to melt rocks roiled in his gut. It didn't matter that Tia was no longer his wife, she should have better taste than to slip into the nearest barbarian's bed and start screaming like a cheap whore.

Pounding on the door, he was determined to stop whatever was going on.

Another wave of moans, louder than the last, set Mason's teeth grinding. Pounding again, he rattled the door hinges. With pleasure, he listened to the Tutsi curse and stumble about.

The door swung open violently. "What the hell do you want?"

The Tutsi commander held a sheet slung low on his waist and an angry scowl.

Mason smiled and looked past the wide shoulders of the African into the room. The bed was a mess of twist-

ed comforter and blankets that hung half on, half off the
queen-sized mattress. Tia was nowhere to be seen. "I
hope I'm not disturbing you."

"You are."

"Then I'll make this brief." He pulled a cigarette from
his battered case and lit it. "I heard that Kabila's head
advisor is in town. Introduce me and I won't bother you
again."

"I told you, I don't need any guns."

Mason put a hand on the closing door. "That may be,
but perhaps Laurent Kabila could use a supplier who can
supply his needs quickly and at a reasonable price."
Blowing smoke, he placed a hand up on the jamb and
leaned forward. It was time to make a sale.

"Think about it. Kabila has played at making war for
decades. I can fix it so he'll never have to deal with con
men who charge astronomical prices and don't always
deliver. You'll be a hero for solving the man's arms supply
issues and I make a fortune. What do you say?"

"I'll think about it," Joseph finally conceded. There
had been times when weapons had been scarce. Even if he
didn't continue with the rebel army, Kabila might be
grateful to resolve future supply issues.

Appeased, Mason took a step back to leave, "Oh by
the way, tell Tia her parents will be here in about twenty
minutes. I'm going to see what breakfast is like in this
dive."

Joseph uttered something unintelligible, then slammed the door.

Mason turned with a smile. This could turn out to be a profitable business trip yet, he thought.

Mason shoved the plate filled with overripe fruit aside and looked toward his aide. "Don't people believe in getting up early to take care of business around here?" he asked irritably.

"I'm afraid, sir, things happen when they happen." Erique gave an amiable smile and finished his breakfast—— if it could be called that.

Mason rose from the table and waved away a fly. He hated eating outside. Didn't know why people thought it was so quaint. He reached for his cigarettes and took note of the passersby in front of the hotel. Most were sickly with worn clothes and blank stares.

He'd slug the first one that came begging for anything.

Suddenly, a black car came up the cobbled street and parked. The windows were dark so he couldn't tell the occupants were Tia's parents until they emerged into the warm Rwandan sunshine.

Mason grinned. He couldn't wait for them to see what their daughter was up to. Pushing open the chipped wrought iron gate, he stepped forward. "Senator Lockhart, Mr. Lockhart," he offered in greeting, "It's a pleasure to see you again."

"Mason." Eliza acknowledged him with a nod as she removed her sunglasses.

Julian Lockhart offered a cool handshake. Not his normal warm self. Mason guessed he must still be steamed about the divorce. A father's prerogative, he supposed.

"Do you know what room Tia is in?" Julian asked.

"113," he said. Rolling around with some barbaric rebel soldier, he wanted to say.

"Well, I've got clothes for her." Eliza raised a small shopping bag. "Poor thing said she's been in the same clothes for more than a week."

Mason didn't mention the two hundred dollars she'd taken from him to buy clothes. Probably had bought some slinky nightgown to turn on her rebel. Holding back his anger, Mason moved aside as the Senator made her way inside the building in her usual all-business stride. He turned to Julian. "Care to join me for coffee? It's better than the food."

Julian looked first toward the front doors. "May as well. I guess I can't see the child 'til she's dressed."

"So, how're things at the Post?" Mason asked, not really caring as he directed the big man back toward the tiny verandah.

"About the same. I've seen a lot of articles come through about this place."

To Mason's delight, Joseph Desiré chose that moment to come out for breakfast. "Ah, look who's here."

Algood's tone was much too cordial. Joseph was immediately on alert. "You still here, Algood?"

"I'd like to introduce you to someone, Joseph. This is Cristiana's father, Julian Lockhart."

Joseph swallowed hard. Tia's father was taller than him by a few inches and considerably heavier. A big man. "Joseph Desiré, sir." Joseph offered a handshake and a slight bow of respect. Suddenly, he felt uncomfortable in his tattered uniform. This was no way to meet his future father-in-law.

"Good to meet you," Julian said, giving his hand a firm shake. His alert eyes traveled down Joseph's attire with interest.

"It seems Mr. Desiré here has been your daughter's escort this past week," Mason continued. "And, after last night, her lover."

Joseph could've ripped the smug grin from Mason's face. Not knowing how to respond, certainly no apology could be made, he remained silent and waited for the elder man to react.

"Am I supposed to be alarmed at that statement, Mason?" Julian waved down a waiter. "Coffee," he ordered. "Joseph?"

"No," Joseph shook his head. "Thank you," he finished, suddenly remembering his manners.

Julian leaned back into his chair. His girth enveloped the narrow wrought iron chair. "Tia is a grown woman.

What she does is no business of mine——or yours, Mason."

A grin threatened to burst upon Joseph's face. He was glad to know Julian held no respect or liking for Tia's ex-husband. Mason's sour look went a long way toward making his day.

"Now Mr. Desiré," Julian turned toward him. "How is it that you and Tia came to be traveling together?"

He had the look of a reporter. Quick, intelligent, inquisitive. Sensing he needed details and not elaboration, Joseph quickly told the story of his saving Tia on the mountain and their brief travels through Cyungugu to Kigali.

"Let me understand this." Julian leaned forward and stared Joseph dead center in the eye. "You saved my daughter and escorted her here?"

"Yes," Joseph answered, wondering what the lingering question was behind the man's eyes.

"Do you feel in need of compensation for your deeds?"

Fury rose within Joseph. He wouldn't think of taking money for Tia's rescue. "Do you mean to disrespect me, sir?"

"Absolutely not," Julian said matter-of-factly. Leaning back to allow the waiter to place the coffee before him, a smile settled on his bearded face. "Just ascertaining what makes you tick, son."

Mason forced himself into the conversation at that moment. "What makes him tick, Mr. Lockhart, is killing Hutus."

"Not anymore." Perfume scented the air as Tia spoke from the doorway.

Moved beyond words, Joseph stared at the vision she made in a flower print summer dress and strappy gold sandals. Her hair was up. Dark, wispy curls framed her creamy brown face at the temples. What a beautiful bride she would make.

"Joseph is going to see Kabila about starting peace talks." She beamed a radiant smile in his direction.

Joseph's blood rushed hot. He didn't remember rising to his feet or seeing Mason and Julian Lockhart do the same. He only knew that the beauty of Cristiana Algood was too striking to take sitting down. He longed to take her back to their room and remove that delicacy of a dress—slowly.

With open arms, Julian walked to his daughter and embraced her. He kissed the top of her head. "Tia baby, thank goodness you're alive." His voice went hoarse with emotion.

Tia clung tighter. "I'm all right. You know I can't die without Mom's permission."

"I heard that, young lady." Her mother's voice held humor as she made her entrance onto the patio. "You always joke when you're tense."

"Looks like you've lost a bit of weight, Cristiana." It was Mason who spoke. Joseph could see lust in the other man's piercing black eyes. If he hadn't sworn off violence, he'd strike him blind.

"Doesn't she look wonderful?" Eliza Lockhart slid past her daughter and husband and pulled her sunglasses down from her head onto her face. "Lucky thing that dress has a tie in back or it would've fallen right off." Smoothing her linen slacks, she sat at the table. "Come on everyone, let's have breakfast."

It touched Joseph's heart to see Tia beam in the presence of her parents. A pang of old grief squeezed his heart as he thought of his own mother.

"We were so grateful you weren't on the boat that sunk." Senator Lockhart studied the one page menu.

"What boat?" Tia asked.

Her dad answered, "The one sailing from Zaire to Tanzania about a week ago. It had Feed the World aid workers on it."

"I missed that boat." Tia closed her eyes remembering the horror. The heat. The sweaty bodies and the screaming. "Everyone was so panicked from the guns—we thought the boat was the quickest way to safety. Did anyone survive?"

"Only half those on board," Julian said softly.

"Damn." Tia whispered with a catch in her voice.

Joseph couldn't watch Tia's obvious distress over the matter. If she'd been killed in that raid... He refused to think about it.

"We didn't know if you were alive or dead until that horrible man, Bolongo, contacted the Embassy," Eliza dropped her menu to grasp her daughter's hand. "Thank God for watching over you."

Perhaps it was the spirit's doing that Joseph caught up with Leonard in time to stop his rampant killing that day. Pure luck more likely, he decided. "I'm sorry, Tia," he offered sincerely.

Her eyes clouded with confusion. "You're sorry? Why? It wasn't your fault that some horrible rebels fired—" Realization silenced her. "It was you?"

"I'd ordered the raid. We were tracking a unit of Hutu militia and thought they had hidden among the refugees at the Uviran camp. That blood-thirsty Bolongo rushed in shooting rather than looking. When I caught up to him, he'd spilled the blood of innocent Uviran refugees all over the beach."

She sat back and stared at him with horror in her eyes. "Why didn't you tell me?"

It was Joseph's turn to be confused. "I thought you knew."

Anger stormed in her eyes. Joseph's gut tightened.

Mason guffawed. "Let me get this straight." His eyes glittered. "You attack Tia and her refugees, then look like a hero later when you show up to save them? Oh, that's rich."

"Apparently, you're the only one who's amused," Julian observed.

A chill of fear traveled Joseph's spine. "It doesn't matter now."

"Of course, it matters, Joseph." Tia's eyes shone with grief and horror. "Anytime someone loses their life, it matters...to me."

Panicked by her accusatory tone, Joseph scraped back from the table in a quick movement. He hadn't bared his soul this morning only to lose her over her high-handed principles.

"I refuse to be blamed for another man's actions. I'm truly sorry those refugees died." The thunder of his pulse raged in his ears. "But I'm grateful that day happened because it brought you into my life."

Tia said nothing, her eyes clouded with hurt.

Her silence convicted him more thoroughly than any words she could've chosen. Joseph felt her slipping away, his newfound happiness fading like the apparition it was.

"That's it." Eliza cut through the tense moment. "I've heard enough of killing innocent people." Eliza waved her hands over the table. "I'm arranging for seats on the first flight out of here."

"No, Mom." Tia grabbed her mother's well-manicured hand. "I can't leave."

Hope rose in Joseph's heart. Perhaps she was reconsidering.

"There are refugees at the border who can't get past their own militiamen to get home," she continued. "I have to help them."

"Is that all?" Joseph demanded, his grief turning to anger. "Is there anything else you want?" He felt as if his entire life hinged on her answer. Balling his fists, he strained to remain in control.

"Not now." Tia spoke quietly, but her refusal reverberated loudly in Joseph's ears.

"Then that's all you'll have." What a fool he'd been for believing in happily-ever-after. "Excuse me. I've got business to conduct." He stood to make his escape.

Mason rose with him. "I certainly hope you're better at business than you are with women, Desiré." He slapped Joseph on the shoulder. "Let me know when your leader arrives."

Shrugging off the man, Joseph strode inside the hotel. The only thing he'd offer Kabila today was his commission as commander of his unit. He was through fighting, nor would he be seeking a position with the government. He didn't want anything but solitude and solace from the new pain searing his soul.

"You sure know how to pick 'em." Eliza took a sip of her husband's coffee and shook her head after Joseph's quick exit.

Tia wasn't in the mood for criticism. "Not now, Mom."

"Yes. Please stop, Senator." Mason stuck his hands in his creased slacks and gave a sickeningly charming smile. "I might get offended."

"How can I make it a certainty?" Eliza looked up at him as if anticipating an answer.

Properly admonished, Mason headed for the door. "It's no wonder Tia turned out the way she did," he growled. "I've got to call my wife to check on my new son."

Mentioning his baby was meant to be a slap to her ego, but strangely, Tia didn't care. Her emotions were in turmoil. Discovering it was Leonard who'd fired on Uvira causing their evacuation shouldn't have surprised her. None of it should have.

But a man's head had exploded only inches from her. Her friends had died on a sunken boat trying to flee Tutsi bullets. She fell down a stupid mountain trying to outrun Joseph and his men. Where did he get the balls to propose after putting her through all that? Did his saving her life make everything all right in his mind? To her, Joseph's silence on the matter felt like deception. And she'd had enough of men's deceit.

"Tia." Her father ran a hand across her shoulders. Here was the only man Tia trusted. One who'd never lied to her about anything. "Let's go to the embassy. You can get some rest and decide what you'd like to do after that."

Tia shook her head. "Thanks, Dad, but I don't have time to rest. Mom," she turned to Eliza. "I need your help."

"With what, baby?"

"Hundreds of thousands of refugees are dying every day. I've got to stay and help."

"Tia, you're only one person. You can't stop a war," her mother argued.

"Exactly, but the United Nations can."

"Oh, no." Eliza shook her head and waved her hands. "We in Congress have already refused to lend more of our men to the U.N. for these foreign wars."

"Political posturing," Julian scoffed. "You all are just trying to gain more power."

"That's not true, Julian. Why should we always be asked to risk our troops in times of trouble? We have no conflict with these people."

"You mean you can't benefit from them."

It was so typical of them to start an argument over principles and politics. Tia remembered the heated dinner conversations they'd had about the combat strategies of Desert Storm and whether or not the US should intervene in the struggle in Bosnia. What else would you expect from a Senator and a newspaper columnist? Strangely, their opposite ideological views seemed to bring them closer together rather than further apart.

Unfortunately, this issue wasn't purely ideological to Tia. It was real and impacted people she'd become quite fond of. "Mom, Dad, listen to me."

Once she had their undivided attention, she made her case. "I've been running for my life for the past week. Traveling with a man named Fidele Zavi and his wife and eight children.

"You ask, Mom, why the U.S. should risk troops to intervene in this civil war and I tell you it's because of people like Fidele. Every day he has to find a way to keep his family safe. Safe from starvation, from illness, from war. He lost the battle yesterday. His wife died of disease. She was too weak to fight it off."

Tia could feel her voice rise as she leaned forward to make her point. "They've been running for two years now. All they want is a chance to get back to some sort of normal life. They want to go home, Mom."

Eliza's eyes were sharp and completely focused on her daughter. "Didn't they reach Kigali with you, dear?"

"Of course, they did. But there are more like them stuck on the border because the Hutu militia won't let them back inside their own country. The U.N., supported by U.S. troops, could open up a safe path to assist these refugees."

"Tia, Congress has debated this with the UN already. I'm afraid there's not a lot of support for sending in US soldiers," Eliza argued.

"Talk them into it," Tia insisted.

"It's much more complicated than th—"

"People are dying, Mother. It doesn't get much simpler than that." Tia couldn't recall ever standing up to her mother as she did now. It felt good to know, finally, what she wanted. "I'm not leaving until the borders are safe for returning Hutus."

"If it means that much to you," her mother's voice came across quietly, "I'll do what I can."

"Thank you." Relieved, Tia relaxed for the first time that morning. "Will you get on it right away?"

Eliza smiled. "You've certainly gotten bossy since you've been here."

It was true. Some sort of internal revolution had happened in the past week. A hidden strength had surfaced from somewhere down deep. "I guess I'm just tired of being scared and helpless. I can't imagine feeling that way for years, like the refugees."

Concern creased Julian's forehead. "You're coming home just as soon as you can?" he asked.

"Yes, Dad." Tia kissed his fuzzy cheek and took comfort in the faint smell of cherry cigar. "When I get home we'll have mocha latté and pastries at Bruegger's. How's that?"

"It's a date, baby." His voice was gentle. "But let me hear from you often."

"I will," Tia assured him.

"Do you need money?" Eliza asked.

"Desperately." Tia brightened. She'd lost everything when her backpack fell over the side of the mountain. "I need a new passport before I can get back, anyway."

"Well, let's get back to the embassy. They can help get everything you need before we go."

"Great." Tia rose to leave with her parents. She glanced back toward the hotel. Last night would live in her dreams until she died. It had been so beautiful, so romantic, so uncomplicated. Until this morning.

She would miss Joseph.

Eleven

The hot sun of mid-day beat down on Joseph as he and three Jeeps holding half his men approached the simple stone building of Laurent Kabila's headquarters.

As he hopped out, two guards at the front of the building moved forward. They were sweating miserably, but not daring to complain.

The older of the two had a raised scar on one cheek which puckered as he smiled. "Bon sieur." One of the men greeted him in French. "Seen a bit of action, Commander?"

Joseph figured his uniform made his appearance as foul as his mood. "More than enough," he replied sourly.

"I'd give anything to be in the thick of it," the younger guard said wistfully.

"Then you're a fool." Joseph pushed past him, not wanting to contribute to any glamorized ideals bouncing around in the boy's head.

"Amani's expecting me," he said as he breezed past the men and inside the old building.

"That he is, Commander," the older man laughed.

The room was hot and muggy. The old ceiling fan did little to cool the hot breeze as it pushed past window bars into the small living area. Amani, Kabila's aide, sipped an iced drink and motioned Joseph to join him. "So, Desiré, you did dare to show your face." Amani's French was polished. Clearly the man had been well-educated.

"Why wouldn't I," Joseph queried.

"Your man, Bolongo had been here to make some important calls. He claimed you were a traitor and had taken up with the Hutus against the rebellion. I offered him two thousand dollars and the rank of commander if he brought you in alive."

Joseph could feel the day going from bad to worse. "You would've rewarded a liar, sir."

"It's not true that you traveled the past week with Hutus?"

"Refugees, not militia," Joseph corrected. "It was Leonard who plotted with the Hutus to make money."

"Indeed?" Amani set down his drink and studied him from behind steepled fingers. "How so?"

"He kidnapped an American woman who traveled with the Hutus and struck a bargain with the militia. He said he would split the $10,000 finder's fee with them if they let him pass safely.

Joseph strode across the room and stared past the bars on the window. "He turned traitor against me. Killed most of my men."

"Where is he now?" Amani asked.

"Dead."

The word hung in the thick air for many seconds before Amani spoke again. "Is there anyone to back up your story?"

"My two men in the hospital."

"Anyone without allegiance to you?" he pressed.

Thanks to Leonard he had to stand and defend his good name. If he weren't already dead... "There is an American arms dealer who could verify my story."

"Good. Anyone else?"

"No." Joseph decided to leave Tia out of it. She didn't want to see him again anyway.

Joseph sat on the arm of the sofa and rubbed his face and eyelids.

"Something wrong, Desiré?" Amani smoothed the collar of his uniform and stood to his full height of five feet-six inches.

"Yes. Something's terribly wrong." He regarded the smaller man with interest. He was, perhaps, the wisest man in the rebellion. Wise enough to be a key leader of the insurrection by whispering advice in Laurent Kabila's ear, thereby avoiding being the target of hate from the Zairians. He might understand what Joseph was about to say. "I fear our people will continue to starve and die of disease because we don't have adequate food stores and health care.

"Afraid that when this battle ends, it will be for nothing. Because the Hutus, angered by the poverty we will impose, will take up arms and begin again."

Amani's boots tapped slowly across the floor and stopped before Joseph. "Don't be ridiculous," he said. "You took Kinsingani, Bukavu, Goma. Despite the distasteful words of your man, Bolongo, Kabila considers you his most valuable commander for clearing half of eastern Zaire. Because of you, Mobutu is shaking in his French Riviera retreat. Once this war is over, the Hutus won't have the resources to organize a coupe."

"For now. What about in five years?"

"They did the same to us."

"My point exactly, sir." Joseph strode the room with passion, "Even as we stand here, the Hutu militiamen Leonard sided with are mounting a raid on this post. Leonard stole the money back he'd promised them. I found it this morning while going through the backpack he carried. You'll need to move out, or prepare to fight."

Amani jolted. "You're certain? How many are there?"

"Hundreds of thousands of them are camped up and down the border of Rwanda and Zaire. I don't know how many will be rallied to attack."

Within seconds, Amani had the entire building on full alert. "There's safe haven in Burundi. Desiré, assume command of these troops and get us there."

"Wouldn't you rather wait for proof of my innocence?" Joseph asked bitterly. "How do you know I won't lead you into a slaughter?"

"I pride myself on being able to read people, Desiré. I would be a fool to believe that boastful Bolongo over you. Let's move."

Adrenaline charged Joseph's veins. Instinctively, a dozen orders came to mind. But, this wasn't what he'd come for.

"I apologize, monsieur. I came to relinquish my command, not accept another." Joseph removed his rifle from his shoulder and let it fall.

Amani seemed deep in thought. With his wire-rimmed glasses, the man looked like a wizened owl.

Taking a deep breath, Amani finally spoke. "I accept your resignation, Desiré."

A little disappointed that it was so easy, Joseph rose to leave.

"I shall leave for Kinshasa from Burundi in two days. Meet me there. Kabila and I have been discussing the possibility of peace talks with Mobutu. You're well-spoken, Desiré. We'll need you in the room for negotiations."

Staring at Amani, Joseph found himself too stunned to talk.

Laughing, the small man sought his abandoned drink and offered a toast. "To you, Desiré." He thrust the liquid back in one gulp and pulled a roll of money from his pocket. "Go find yourself a few suits worthy of your new station. And by the gods, if you're not coming with us, see that you don't get killed."

"Yes, sir." Joseph accepted the money, not able to believe the turn of events, nor did he know quite how to feel about them. Maybe being able to use his brain rather brawn would keep his mind off Tia. She was tucked away in the American Embassy by now. It surprised him to see her parents leave today without her. Why had she stayed?

He'd go to Kinshasa, assist with peace talks and hopefully feel more humane for doing so. With a long deep breath, he studied the sky of his home. For the moment, it was quiet and blue. Only the faintest traces of clouds could be seen. Closing his eyes, he thought back to his youth when it was always like this. If it had been that way once, it could be so again.

Hope filled him. Joseph offered himself a sad smile. Damned if he could shake Tia's fairy tales.

It would've been so easy to leave. The embassy had her new passport in a matter of hours. But Tia's heart would be just as broken, her mind just as bewildered as it was now.

She hadn't slept for the past three nights. Thoughts of Joseph and his sweet words and sincere proposal warred with visions of him slaying Zairian soldiers and the stained red beach of Uvira.

Between tossing and twisting her sheets last night, she realized how much she loved the Tutsi rebel. Joseph lit her system like fireworks on the Fourth and it was precisely that which frightened her most. What if she agreed to stay with him, to be his wife? They would never have children. In what year of their marriage would he decide to discard her? Where would she go to heal the wounds a second time? There were only so many continents in the world, after all.

"Coward." She sank against the pillows of the comfortable bed. She wasn't angry about Uvira. It was an excuse, her anger, to keep Joseph at arm's length, to keep him from hurting her as Mason had.

Tia sighed. She was to meet Fidele and his children at their home. Rising, she patted the paper with directions in her pocket. Her body felt heavy with depression as she opened the door.

Leaning against a wall near the door, looking completely gorgeous, was Mason. If possible, her mood turned more sour. "Mason. What do you want?"

"Rudeness doesn't become you, Cristiana." Without awaiting invitation, he entered her room. "I don't know what's happened to alter your once perky personality—"

"Try a wicked divorce." Tia slammed the door, tired of Mason's insults. Emotionally, she'd gone through too much with Joseph and her patience was non-existent. "And an ex-husband who preys on my weaknesses at every turn to make me feel inferior. Like I'm dirt beneath his feet."

Warning rose in Mason's eyes. "That's quite enough," he admonished. "I didn't come here for verbal sparring. Your parents dished out plenty the other day."

"Then why are you here?" Tia crossed her arms and looked Mason directly in the eyes for the first time in years.

"I need your assistance with a business matter."

"You can't be serious." Tia looked for deceit in his expression.

Mason pulled out a cigarette and tapped it on his gold case.

"Light that when you're gone," Tia asserted. She'd never appreciated his blowing smoke in her face.

Eyes narrowed, Mason slowly moved the stick to his lips. "I'll hold it here for safekeeping, how's that?"

Tia shrugged. No need making a bigger deal of it.

"I'd hate to come here and not make a single bill in profit," Mason began.

"Is what you do legal?" Tia countered.

"It is when you're working on behalf of the United States government." Mason winked.

A million thoughts barraged Tia's brain, all with one conclusion. "This is the government contract work you do? Selling arms to people who have no better sense than to kill one another?" Amazing, Mason and her own government were responsible for keeping this war going in Africa. "You could sell farm equipment, sponsor educational efforts and health care."

"That's not what the leaders here want." Mason played with the cigarette in his mouth. Waggling it up and down with his tongue. "Not what they pay for."

"What sense does it make to give them weapons and then send in aid workers to bandage them up and feed them?"

"Ironic, ain't it?" He laughed. "Why do you think it took so long for Congress to finally offer up our boys to help out here?"

Tia was happy her mother had been so persuasive. Talks of the US sending troops to assist the UN in escorting Hutu and Zairian refugees had begun the moment she got back home. She hoped it didn't take much longer to deploy them.

"You're crazy." She looked at him hard, wondering if she'd really known him at all. "How do you sleep at night, Mason?"

Removing the unlit cigarette from his mouth, Mason rounded on Tia. "I only sell the damn things. I don't pull the trigger."

"That's a cop-out and you know it." Tia went to the window protected by bars and looked out at the guarded compound. "All this security wouldn't be necessary if you'd just let these people run out of bullets."

"Right," Mason scoffed. "If I don't sell them, there's always someone else, some other country to supply them. Jump off your mythical high-horse, Tia, and join the rest of us in the real world, would you?" He placed a hand on her shoulder to turn her around.

"Your rebel boyfriend was supposed to arrange a meeting with Laurent Kabila's man for me. All I need is for you to call him up and ask him to move a little faster on it." He moved in closer. "I know he'll listen to you. You've got him whipped like meringue. I could see it in his eyes."

She remembered Joseph's eyes, the pain in them when she dismissed him in one fell judgment. Today, she wished she could take back her words.

As for Mason, nothing lived in his eyes, no emotion, only cold calculations of how to make himself richer. There was a time she'd believed his eyes sexy. No more.

"Help me out," he continued, "and I'll cut you in for a percentage of the profits." He flashed his signature smile expecting it would work magic as it used to.

"Not today. Go charm somebody else, Mason. I can't help you."

In four quick steps, she was across the room, holding the door open for him. "Please, leave."

Unhurried, Mason met Tia at the door. He all but leered at her as he looked her up and down. "You do look good, you know?"

She knew. It was all she could do to walk past a mirror and not twist and turn in awe over her new figure. Never in her life had she been so thin. Still not as skinny as supermodel Cindy, but her stomach was now flat and her thighs didn't rub together. Hanging out in Zaire and walking the mountain paths had done more for her weight loss efforts than six months of health club workouts. "Eat your heart out."

Tia opened the door wider. "I can't help you with Joseph. In case you weren't paying attention, we're not on good terms."

"I noticed." Mason stepped closer and pushed the door closed.

His cologne nearly suffocated her. "What are you doing?" she asked.

"Since you're not getting it on with the African warrior anymore," his hands roamed her breasts freely, "I thought I'd help you work out any sexual frustrations you might have."

"You've got some nerve, Mason." With both hands she thrust him off her. "I'm not desperate enough to get back in bed with you."

Running both hands over his short-cropped waves, Mason struggled to regain his demeanor. "Just trying to do you a favor."

For a moment, his words stung. He was back in the business of making her feel worthless, until she remembered the lust in his eyes. His hands hadn't groped her as if she was a charity case, but like a woman who'd driven a man to lust. It was she who had the upper hand here. "Let's not fool ourselves, it would've been me doing the favor. Go back to your wife and child."

It was a crooked smile he offered. One full of smug humor. "You got the birth announcement?"

"Yes. We've been through this, remember?"

"I thought you'd like to know."

"Why? To torment me, throw my shortcomings in my face one last time?" Hurt and angry, Tia dared him to come within slapping distance. "Well, it worked. Are you happy now?"

The smile wavered, then dropped from his face. Mason hung his head and sighed. "No, I'm not happy. Haven't been for a long time. And you, of all people, should be able to tell." Hands on his hips, he paced the ornate rug. "I don't mean to torment you, Tia. I never have."

"Could've fooled me." Disgusted, she went to the window and looked past the bars to the well-tended lawn. "I came here to escape you. I was tired of feeling bad about myself and having everyone pity me for being thrown over for your perfect new wife. A wife who could give you a son." Pain slashed through her heart when she said it.

Mason sighed and sank onto the bed. "I wish I could say I had a good reason for the things I've said and done to you since our divorce." He lifted eyes filled with true emotion. "I don't."

Tia shook her head, more confused than ever. "Then, why—?"

"Because I wanted you."

Stunned, she stood in silence, waiting for him to continue.

"I wanted you...and a child."

"We could've adopted."

He shook his head. "One of my own blood," his tone was adamant. "I got angry with you when you didn't get pregnant. Six years was a long time to sow seeds without benefit of a crop. Then I got frightened thinking it might've been me who was infertile." His pause was weighty. "Cindy happened by at a weak moment. And when she got pregnant...I got so excited..."

Slowly, the picture came together in her head. "You got her pregnant and wanted to give your child your name, right?"

His Adam's apple bobbed in his throat. "Yes. My child wasn't going to be born illegitimate."

"How noble." Placing a hand to her throat, Tia struggled to keep tears from mingling with her anger. "You tossed me out like Tuesday's garbage because you wanted a child more than you wanted me."

"No," his voice was low and soft. "I loved you. Never stopped. I just realized it too late. Cindy had started making plans, we'd signed up for childbirth classes—"

Tia pushed words past her tightening throat. "It was wrong, Mason."

Hanging his head once again, he nodded. "I know it was. I said hateful things because I wanted to believe it was all your fault. That it was you who was inadequate and drove me to do what I did. And with every hurtful word I've thrown at you, I've become less and less a man."

Floored by his confession, Tia let his words settle into her conscious thoughts. "So, you didn't leave because I wasn't woman enough?"

"Hell, no. Is that what you thought?"

"It's what you've led me to believe."

He stared at the rug intently as he spoke, "I guess I went too far trying to make myself feel good about cheating on you."

The following moments passed in silence. Tia felt one of the two loads she carried lift quietly from her heart. "Thank you for telling me," she said softly.

Turning from the window, she crossed the room to stand before her ex-husband. Taking his hands, she pulled until he rose to his feet. "I needed to hear that."

"That's it?" He seemed genuinely surprised. "I'm forgiven?"

Tia nodded. "Only if you're being sincere and not trying to put me off guard to help you."

He grinned. "I guess I deserve that." He bent to kiss her forehead. "You've always been a better person than me, Tia. Don't ever change."

Mason held one of her hands as he walked to the door. "Care to join me for breakfast?" He shrugged and smiled. "Now that we're friends."

She might've been twenty pounds lighter, but her appetite was relentless. "Only if you keep your hands to yourself."

"To be both honest and a gentleman all in one day goes against my nature, dear lady," he expounded theatrically. "But, you have my word." He held up both palms to prove it.

Tia laughed. "Come on. There's a restaurant just down the street."

Having this tenuous friendship with Mason was just what she needed to get her mind off Joseph. Ironically, it had taken traveling thousands of miles across an ocean for her and Mason to reconcile their differences. In a way, she felt sorry for him, he had a loveless marriage. Hopefully, the child would make up for it.

Jealousy constricted Joseph's gut as Tia and Mason entered the restaurant. They laughed easily with each other, chatted amiably. Had her bastard of an ex-husband gotten back into her good graces so quickly?

It took only a moment for their eyes to meet across the small, crowded restaurant. Cursing under his breath, Joseph wished he hadn't stayed for a second cup of coffee. He'd hoped to leave for Kinshasa today without further complications.

Rising from the table, he braced for their approach.

"You look nice, Joseph." Tia seemed supremely uncomfortable as she acknowledged his new suit.

Good, he thought. If he was miserable, the least she could be was nervous. "Thank you. So do you, Tia." Too good for his heart to take. "I was just leaving. Feel free to take my table."

Mason pulled out a chair for Tia. "No need to rush off, Desiré. I was hoping to talk with you about that introduction to Kabila."

"Mason!" Tia threw an alarmed look at him.

"I told you," he said with patience, "you're a better person than I'll ever be."

Joseph watched the exchange with interest. Judging by Tia's expression, it seemed Algood was about to lose a little ground with his ex-wife. Unfortunately, Joseph would have to get him off the hook. "I'll save you some time and energy, Algood. Kabila doesn't need anymore guns. We're on our way to Kinshasa to arrange peace talks with Mobutu Sese Seko."

"What makes you think Mobutu will sit down for talk? This war's been going on for years at his insistence," Mason countered.

"He's old. He's ill." Joseph countered. "He's got just as many enemies inside his camp as outside. The time is right."

"Good for you, Joseph." Tia rose awkwardly to stand before him. The air went electric with her so close. She smelled of perfume and powder. Her raven waves were twisted up carelessly, with curls bouncing at the top of her head. She wore jeans that hugged curvy hips and a tank top revealing a heavenly portion of breast. Every male hormone in his body went on alert.

"I know it doesn't mean much, but I'm very proud of you." Nervously, she wet her lips.

He barely heard her words, though her mouth had his undivided attention.

Mason said something, but Joseph didn't hear. He took a step closer to her.

Tia cleared her throat, but stopped talking. Her big brown eyes spoke volumes about the desire she wanted to bury, but couldn't.

Joseph wanted to touch her, had to, one last time before he left. Slowly, he pulled her toward him, pressing her warm curves tight to his body, grateful she offered no resistance. So good, he thought. She feels so good.

He covered her mouth then with a long, slow, satisfying kiss. Patiently he explored her mouth, logging the sweet taste of her to memory as a starving man relishes every bite of his last meal. Her arms were around his neck, her sweet moans fueling his arousal.

Only the vague recollection that they were in a public place kept Joseph from making his caresses more intimate and his kiss any longer. Pulling back, loathe to break their connection, Joseph continued to hold her in his arms.

It took a moment before he could find his voice. "If you're ever in Kinshasa," he spoke so only she could hear, "and you want to save someone's life...I know a desperate man who'll be waiting."

Tears filled her eyes, but she didn't speak.

Knowing he couldn't stay longer without throwing her over his shoulder and hauling her off to the capital of Zaire with him, Joseph released her. Tossing a few bills onto the table, he left without turning back. He couldn't help but believe he'd just left the best part of his life behind.

Tia held back her tears, but sat quickly to let the room finish spinning. Joseph was gone and she'd done nothing to stop him.

Angrily, Mason scraped a chair across the scarred wood floor. "It's a damn good thing he left. You two were going at it like a couple of teenagers in the back of a theater. It's broad daylight, for God's sake."

"Sorry if I embarrassed you, Mason." Tia put fingers to her tingling lips and let her heart finish breaking.

Mason rubbed a hand over his face. "What the hell do you expect from me? You think it's easy watching another man kiss your wife?"

She shot him a telling look.

"Okay, okay," he conceded. "My ex-wife." Picking up a menu, he attempted to change the subject. "Tell you what, let's get something to eat. Apparently, I won't be doing business with the Tutsis today."

Tia shook her head. Her appetite was gone. "I'm not hungry any more." Wanting to be alone, she headed for the door. "I'm going to see Fidele. I'll take a cab."

Dropping the menu, Mason caught up with her on the sidewalk. "You don't look too good. Maybe you should see your friend later."

Tia shook her head, not trusting herself to talk. She hailed a cab from the busy line of cars and people crowding the street. "I'll see you later, huh?" she said to Mason.

"Yeah. Take care." He closed the cab door.

Tia told the driver where she was going, then settled inside the hot interior. Heated air struggled to circulate as the car crawled in heavy traffic. Everything seemed stifled, like her emotions.

It took twenty minutes to clear the inner portion of the city. Tia hadn't realized the city would be as modern as any American one she'd visited. Restaurants, hotels, stores, anything you would want could be found in the high rise buildings and store-lined streets.

Outside the city, the buildings wore the scars of war. Huge portions of once livable space had been blown from homes that lined the littered streets like skeletons. Bullet holes pocked the faces of those that still had all four walls and mended tarps served as Band-Aids for tattered roofs.

The cab slowed. A child ran happily past, jumping over pipes, kitchen sinks, toilets. It was Denis.

Tia couldn't help smiling at the sight of her little friend. "Hey, Denis," she said exiting the cab.

"Hey, hey, hey, Tia!" He turned in a full circle and hopped and ran his way over to her.

Tia lifted him and hugged him tight. "What's got you so jumpy today?" she asked, planting a sloppy kiss on his smooth cheek.

"Dis our house." He waved a hand toward the one-story, windowless home. From where she stood, it looked as if it had been spared major damage. It had a roof. It had four walls. "Come on, Tia."

Allowing herself to be dragged through the hole where a door had once stood, Tia could feel the weight of sadness lifting. Once inside, she could see the place had been gutted of all lighting fixtures. Interior doors hung at odd angles or were full of holes. The sun shone brightly down upon the kitchen from the gaping hole in a roof that at first glance had looked sound.

The Zavi girls had busied themselves with dusting and sweeping while the boys hauled out broken furniture. All were singing, clearly happy to be home.

Fidele came bustling in from a rear door, a rusted hammer in hand. "Tia." An elfin grin spread across the man's face. "Welcome to my home."

Arms out, he turned in a circle, celebrating his home-coming, joining his children in song.

Tia let the jumping Denis down and hummed the catchy tune. She didn't understand the words, but the meaning was clearly one of joy.

Within hours, the home was as clean as it could get without cleaning products. They all found it amazing that the water was connected and operable. Tia found pots and pans in the kitchen, but little else. She was starving and knew the Zavis were as well. "Let's go to the store and get something for dinner," she said to Kisha, the oldest girl.

All eyes lit up at the talk of food. No cabs could be hailed here, so they began the long walk toward town. As they neared the city, men, women and children dressed in rags stood in clumps with their hands out.

"Please give. We need food," they said as Tia and Kisha walked past.

Tia's heart nearly broke. There were so many who needed help, she wanted to give to as many as she could. "Oh, Kisha, this is horrible."

Kisha only walked past with her head hung. "Mama used to say the same." She spoke with the same sweet pitch as her mother, but her English was as good as her father's. "She would buy boxes of oatmeal and cereals to give to as many as she could," she continued.

"Then we'll do the same," Tia decided with a nod.

Tia felt like Santa Claus as she passed out boxes of food to the starving dozens from the rear of the only convertible cab she could find.

It was a good idea to keep the Zavis food in the trunk, otherwise, she would've given that as well. She'd had every intention of paying Mason back his two hundred dollars, but decided he needed to give something to the country besides guns—even if he didn't know it.

Their dinner was satisfying and enjoyed by all the neighbors on Zavi's street. Dancing in the street began and singing and jumping in unison, the Hutus celebrated being home.

It was midnight before Tia crawled into bed at the hotel. She wondered if Joseph slept. His room was only down the hall a few doors. Remembering the feel of his arms around her, she fell into a sound sleep.

The next morning's news reports heralded the deployment of U.S. troops to Zaire and Rwanda to assist the U.N. in escorting Hutu refugees home.

Tia blew a sigh at the ceiling. It was time to go home.

Twelve

Joseph stood on the deck of the ship. Today they would make history. If Mobutu Sese Seko arrived, peace talks would begin. If he failed to show, Laurent Kabila planned to appoint himself President.

Either way, Joseph knew his position in Kabila's cabinet was assured. He'd talked for long hours these past few weeks with Kabila, telling him his ideas for a new Zaire. Kabila had plans as well. He'd decided to change the name of the country when he took power. His new country would be called the Democratic Republic of the Congo.

Armed soldiers stood guard at every door of the ship, prepared to do battle if the peace talks failed to bring about a non-violent resolution. Joseph nearly laughed at the irony.

The air was fresh, cool. No land could be seen for miles. At least here, on this portion of neutral ocean, a struggle wouldn't impact any innocent civilians, save the French Nationals who'd arrived to back Mobutu. They wanted him to stay in power because he'd been giving them mineral rights to Zaire's largest treasure at bargain prices. They didn't care that the money served only to line the president's pockets.

Of course, there was the American, as well. Joseph still didn't know how Mason Algood had managed to find him in Kinshasa. Even now, a smile, ever arrogant and confident, played on the man's face as his expensive shoes struck the wooden deck.

"Nervous, Desiré?" Mason asked, taking the last puff of his cigarette before tossing it into the gray, green ocean.

"What's to be nervous about? Mobutu won't show."

"Well, if he does, we're ready, eh?" Mason looked proudly around at the men bearing arms.

Joseph gave him a noncommittal grunt. Hopefully, his warring days were over. But then what?

"What's next for you, Desiré?" Mason asked, as if reading his mind.

"There's much work to be done in Zaire." A thousand ideas bounced around his head. Rebuilding neighborhoods, establishing schools, finding jobs for all Zairians, not just the Tutsis.

"Maybe so." Mason tugged on the waist of his slacks. "But you know what they say about all work and no play?"

"What?" Joseph had no idea what the man was talking about.

"Find a woman, have a family, settle down." Mason gestured grandly. "Enjoy life a little."

"No time." Joseph stared out to sea, trying not to let the raw emotion within him show. How could he enjoy anything without Tia?

Mason leaned on the rail, matching Joseph's position. "You're still pretty torn up about Tia leaving, aren't you?"

"You're a mind reader as well as an arms dealer?" Joseph bit back. "The last thing I want to do is talk about a woman with her ex-husband."

Nodding, Mason pursed his lips reflectively. "Good point." He stood quietly for moment before saying more. "I saw her last week, you know?"

Joseph couldn't help the flash of jealousy that ran through him. "How is she?"

"Sick."

"She's ill?" Panic raced through Joseph's system like a shock wave.

"Not seriously." Mason shrugged. "My wife went through the same thing. Puking up every morning."

Joseph frowned. "Are you being intentionally vague to make me angry?"

Mason shuffled around a bit. "No. I'm trying to get over the embarrassment of you being able to do in one week what I couldn't in six years."

Joseph suddenly realized what he was talking about. "She's pregnant?" He grinned.

Mason nodded.

He slapped the smaller man on the back heartily. "Telling me had to hurt like hell, huh, Algood?"

Offering a sheepish grin, Mason confessed, "I'm actually kind of happy it happened. She'll be so happy when she knows."

"Now you're confusing me again." Joseph stepped back. "How could you know she's pregnant when she doesn't?"

"I've lived with a pregnant woman. I know one when I see one," Mason assured him. "It'd be a shame if she had to go through it all alone."

Joseph offered his hand.

Mason gripped it firmly.

"Thanks for telling me," Joseph gave an extra shake before releasing Mason's hand. "I used to attend school in D.C. All I need is an address to find her."

"Here." Mason slid the business card from his pocket. "She's working at Feed the World headquarters downtown. I'm not sure of her home address."

"That's as it should be," Joseph teased.

"See ya', champ. Good luck in the talks if Mobutu ever shows. I've gotta head back." Mason turned on an expensive Italian leather heel and headed for the small boat floating alongside the huge cruiseliner.

Joseph gave him an absentminded wave as he thought of all the things he had to arrange to get to America. It was probably his imagination, but the sky seemed to have gotten bluer, clearer. Whether the peace talks got under way or not, it was going to be a great day.

❖❖❖

Tia grabbed her keys from the little table by her front door and scanned the living room of her condo. It felt as if she was missing something. Truth was, she'd felt like that since she'd returned to the States two months ago. Hard as she tried, she couldn't shake Africa—or its people. She hated not being able to call Fidele to find out how he was doing.

Shaking her head, Tia pushed back the sad tug on her heart. She'd be late to work if she didn't get moving. They'd been happy to see her safe and alive when she'd returned to Feed The World, but not so happy they didn't expect a good day's work out of her now that she was on the payroll.

It was a clear day, though the traffic was horrendous. Still, Tia enjoyed watching the tall, lush trees stretching toward the sky as she made her daily trek from Maryland to the heart of D.C.

Grabbing her briefcase and high heels from the seat next to her, she exited the parking garage and walked the long blocks to her office. Feed The World was on the seventh floor. Tia felt a pitching in her stomach and rise of queasiness as the elevator door "dinged" and opened.

"Morning, Miss Algood," Georgia, the pretty chocolate-colored receptionist, sang out. "Are you all right?" Her blazing smile turned to concern.

"Yes. I'm fine." Tia attempted a smile. She managed to drop her things in her office before running to the bathroom and losing the toast and tea she'd had for break-fast.

Tia emerged ten minutes later a little lightheaded, but feeling better.

"I'm not being nosy," the slight man with blond hair said, "but that's three times this week, you've run for the bathroom like it's your lost lover."

"Michael, don't you have better things to do than follow me around the halls?" Tia didn't know why she was so irritated all of a sudden.

"Just looking after your welfare. Since we both escaped Zaire with our lives, barely, I have this bond with you I can't explain."

He said it with such a cheery voice and bright smile Tia couldn't help but shake her head and smile back. "I was relieved you didn't drown after that boat capsized," she said in earnest.

"Yeah," he said absently. "Say. If you're hungry for lunch, why don't we make it a date?"

Lunch. Ugh. The last thing she wanted to think about was food. "Well, I—uh."

"Come on. I have a surprise for you," he pleaded.

"Sure. Okay." Tia went inside her office as Michael all but danced down the hall. Putting a hand to her tender stomach, she flipped through her organizer to see what time she'd made her appointment with the doctor. She was concerned she'd gotten malaria or a bad case of the flu while in Rwanda. She hadn't felt well since her return.

2:00PM.

Not feeling like checking phonemail or e-mail at the moment, she turned in her chair and looked out over the city. The concrete and glass contrasted violently with the lush forests and green meadows of Zaire and Rwanda. She'd been so terrified while she was there, it just now occurred to her how absolutely beautiful the countries had been.

The gorgeous orange and purple streaked sunsets. The morning dew sitting like raindrops on the huge green leaves of the brush. The nights that fell like a dark curtain sprinkled with stars as she'd fallen asleep in Joseph's arms.

Maybe she should've made an appointment with a shrink instead of a general practitioner. She had to have been crazy to leave Joseph. She closed her eyes and wished herself back there.

"Joseph," she whispered. "I miss you so much."

"Then marry me."

Tia jumped from her chair at the sound of his sexy baritone. He filled her door with his broad shoulders and wide stance. She was dreaming. Had to be.

Her heart raced as his warm smile and determined gaze captured her once again.

"Why did you run from me?" Joseph moved inside the room.

Tia couldn't find words, couldn't do anything but stare at her African god in his expensive dark blue suit.

"Are you surprised?" Michael poked out from behind Joseph with an impish gleam in his eyes. "I wanted to wait until lunchtime, but Joseph insisted on seeing you now."

Nodding like an idiot—a speechless idiot—Tia continued to stare as Joseph moved around her desk to take her in his arms.

Melting under his kiss, Tia felt the room spin and her body awaken. His mouth coerced hers open and sought her tongue with his own.

"Ahhh, suki, suki, now."

It was Georgia's voice. Tia recognized it, but didn't acknowledge the receptionist's presence.

"I guess I'll hold Miss Thang's calls for a while."

"Good idea," Michael attempted a whisper.

Tia vaguely recalled a door closing before getting lost in the wonder of Joseph Desiré. Even when he ended the kiss, she held tight to his neck and buried her face in his chest. He smelled wonderful.

"Have you enjoyed hot baths and soft beds while you've been here?" His voice was lighthearted and teasing.

"Yes." She smiled into his jacket.

"I heard you say you missed me. Is that true?" he baited.

"Yes." Tia clung tighter to him. He was going to ask again. She could feel it coming.

"I'm flattered, but you should've known I'd find you."
His hands traveled up and down her back in a light massage. "Should've known I could never let you go."

"Oh, Joseph. I don't know what to say to you." She
stepped back now and looked into his dark eyes. She was
certain she could see his soul in their depths. "I won't let
you throw away your life on me. Someone else..." She
couldn't say the words, couldn't even entertain the thought
of another woman being with him. Being his wife.

His gaze never wavered as he stared back at her. "My
life is with you, Tia. Within you." His smile was warm as
it touched her lips briefly. "I'll have many sons by you."

Tia's heart ached. "Haven't you been paying attention?
I can't have children."

"Oh but you can." His large hand warmed her stomach and rested on her womb. "My mother visited me in
a dream. She told me that my seed was planted deep within you. It grows even now."

Tia was certain the only thing growing beneath his
hand was her lust. The Tutsis were very spiritual people.
She knew she couldn't laugh away his vision or what he
thought he'd heard. But she had to make him listen to reason. "What if your mother is wrong? What if you wanted it to be true so badly that you dreamed it up on your
own?"

"What will it take to prove it to you?"

"A blood test, I guess."

"How shall we arrange it?"

She was going to the doctor this afternoon anyway. She could request a blood test, couldn't she? "I'll have one done this afternoon. How's that?"

"Perfect." He backed away toward the door. "I'll be attending meetings with the Zairian Ambassador until five o'clock. I'll be back to pick you up then. We'll go shopping for your wedding gown."

"Don't you want to wait for the test results before you go planning anything?" Tia leaned across her desk to shout at his retreating form.

"I know the results. But it wouldn't matter either way. You will be my wife." He stopped long enough to give her a lustful grin that sent her head spinning. Then he was gone.

Tia collapsed in her chair and Georgia came racing in with a thousand questions shooting from her bright red lips. "Who was that gorgeous hunk of man, child?" she finally asked.

Tia shrugged her shoulders and shook her head. "My next husband, apparently." There was no stopping the smile that took over.

"Ooh, you lucky woman. Mmm, Mmm, Mmm." Georgia fanned herself and uttered something totally unintelligible as she walked back out.

❖❖❖

Tia returned from the doctor at three-thirty with a promise of the pregnancy test results by five. It was five-fifteen and the nurse hadn't called.

Joseph sat across from her wearing a smug smile. "The Ambassador has agreed to interview you for a position with the Kinshasa embassy. Or, you could teach, since you have such a way with children. Either way, I knew you would want to work when we return to Zaire."

What was he saying? Tia couldn't pay attention for watching the phone. "Call." She leaned over the piece of black plastic wishing for a green light. "Call."

"We could go out to dinner and call them tomorrow—"

"No." Tia held up a hand, nerves jangling. "I'll call them."

As her hand covered the receiver, it rang. Her heart nearly leapt from her chest. "Hello." Squeezing her eyes shut, she prayed for good news.

"Miss Algood?"

"Yes."

"This is Nurse Cooke calling with your results."

"Yes. Please continue." She couldn't breathe.

"The blood test was positive. Congratulations, you're going to be a mommy."

"Thank you. Thank you. Oh, thank you." Tia opened her eyes and looked at Joseph through tears. "I'm pregnant."

Jumping to his feet, he took her hands. "I know."

Climbing over her desk, Tia fell into his arms and kissed his face all over. "I'll marry you, Joseph. I will."

He carried her to the door while she hugged and kissed him some more. "You say that as if you had a choice."

And, the truth of it was, she didn't have a choice. Her heart belonged to Joseph and his country completely. Always had, even while she tried to deny it. Nothing in the States could compete with the experiences she'd had in Africa—good or bad. She would go back now, to her new country, with her new husband and make a difference. A real difference.

About the Author

Tanya. T. Henderson is an Assistant Vice President at a nationally known financial institution. Tanya's writing career began when she won First Place in the contemporary romance category of the Pikes Peak Writers Conference in 1995. Encouraged by the success of African-American authors Terry McMillan and Walter Mosely, Tanya writes for an ethnic audience. Her books are written with lively plots and interesting characters; her primary purpose being to entertain her readers and make faces of color a consistent presence in the romance genre. Tanya's first novel, *Passion*, was published by Genesis Press in 1997 and has since been reissued in mass market format by Ballantine. She lives in Texas with her husband and two daughters.

Heartbeat
by Stephanie Bedwell-Grime
ISBN 1-58571-008-3
$8.95

Carmen Day has a job she loves in the Medical Photography Department at Royal Hospital. Her comfortable work world is threatened, however, when downsizing expert Max Deveraux announces plans to shut the department down in a cost-cutting measure. When Carmen finds out and storms into Max's office to demand he reconsider, he is so impressed with her spirit and drive that he does—somewhat. He gives Carmen one week to convince him to leave the department open.

Carmen's best friend gives what seems like sound advice: Make Max fall in love with you, and you'll save your job. Thus begins a tangled web of hospital politics and romance, and when Carmen realizes that she's lost her own heart, that this game of seduction is more than a game for her, she learns that Max has romanced all the women he's fired in the past.

Has Carmen truly won Max's heart? Or will she just be another statistic in the ledger of "Max the Axe," the most ruthless downsizing expert in his field?

Secret Library Vol. 2
A Brush With Passion
by Cassandra Colt
ISBN 1-58571-011-3
$8.95

Nina Ashton has come to L.A. with hopes of land-
ing a prestigious position as a skilled art conser-
vator. She settles instead for a less-than-perfect
job working for Marcus Pike, owner of Pike Fine
Art Services, Inc.

When Nina learns that thieves have made off with
several paintings and damaged others belonging
to the wealthy collector, Raffy Whitman, she
decides to pay Raffy a visit herself to give an
estimate for the cost of restoring the damaged
paintings. Raffy is instantly captivated by her and
convinces Nina to come to work for his Whitman
Art Foundation. Thus begins an exciting liaison
between the two that takes Nina to Paris and
Switzerland in search of a valuable stolen paint-
ing, and into the beds of the men who they sus-
pect may have acquired it.

Order your favorite Genesis
Press titles directly from us!
Visit our web site for the latest
information
www.genesis-press.com
or call toll-free
1.888.463.4461

INDIGO: Sensuous Love Stories *Order Form*

ail to:
enesis Press, Inc.
15 3rd Avenue North
olumbus, MS 39701

Visit our website at

http://www.genesis-press.com

ame————————————————————————

ddress———————————————————————

ity/State/Zip—————————————————————

1999 INDIGO TITLES

ty	Title	Author	Price	Total
	Somebody's Someone	Sinclair LeBeau	$8.95	
	Interlude	Donna Hill	$8.95	
	The Price of Love	Beverly Clark	$8.95	
	Unconditional Love	Alicia Wiggins	$8.95	
	Mae's Promise	Melody Walcott	$8.95	
	Whispers in the Night	Dorothy Love	$8.95	
	No Regrets (paperback reprint)	Mildred Riley	$8.95	
	Kiss or Keep	D.Y. Phillips	$8.95	
	Naked Soul (paperback reprint)	Gwynne Forster	$8.95	
	Pride and Joi (paperback Reprint)	Gay G. Gunn	$8.95	
	A Love to Cherish (paperback reprint)	Beverly Clark	$8.95	
	Caught in a Trap	Andree Jackson	$8.95	
	Truly Inseparable (paperback reprint)	Wanda Thomas	$8.95	
	A Lighter Shade of Brown	Vicki Andrews	$8.95	
	Cajun Heat	Charlene Berry	$8.95	

se this order form
r call:

1-888-INDIGO1

(1-888-463-4461)

TOTAL _____
Shipping & Handling _____
(**$3.00 first book $1.00 each additional book**)

TOTAL Amount Enclosed _____
MS Residents add 7% sales tax

INDIGO *Backlist Titles*

QTY	TITLE	AUTHOR	PRICE	TOTA
	A Love to Cherish	Beverly Clark	$15.95 HC*	
	Again My Love	Kayla Perrin	$10.95	
	Breeze	Robin Hampton	$10.95	
	Careless Whispers	Rochelle Alers	$8.95	
	Dark Embrace	Crystal Wilson Harris	$8.95	
	Dark Storm Rising	Chinelu Moore	$10.95	
	Entwined Destinies	Elsie B. Washington	$4.99	
	Everlastin' Love	Gay G. Gunn	$10.95	
	Gentle Yearning	Rochelle Alers	$10.95	
	Glory of Love	Sinclair LeBeau	$10.95	
	Indiscretions	Donna Hill	$8.95	
	Love Always	Mildred E. Riley	$10.95	
	Love Unveiled	Gloria Green	$10.95	
	Love's Deception	Charlene A. Berry	$10.95	
	Midnight Peril	Vicki Andrews	$10.95	
	Naked Soul	Gwynne Forster	$15.95 HC*	
	No Regrets	Mildred E. Riley	$15.95 HC*	
	Nowhere to Run	Gay G. Gunn	$10.95	
	Passion	T.T. Henderson	$10.95	
	Pride and Joi	Gay G. Gunn	$15.95 HC*	
	Quiet Storm	Donna Hill	$10.95	
	Reckless Surrender	Rochelle Alers	$6.95	
	Rooms of the Heart	Donna Hill	$8.95	
	Shades of Desire	Monica White	$8.95	
	Truly Inseparable	Mildred Y. Thomas	$15.95 HC*	
	Whispers in the Sand	LaFlorya Gauthier	$10.95	
	Yesterday is Gone	Beverly Clark	$10.95	

* indicates Hard Cover

Total for Books _____
Shipping and Handling _____
($3.00 first book $1.00 each additional book)